THE MARTIN CULVER SERIES

THE SECRET OF BLUE SCORPION KEY

MALCOM MASSEY

The Secret of Blue Scorpion Key

Malcom Massey

June 30, 2023
Melbourne, Florida

Copyright June 2023 by Malcom Massey

ISBN: 9798391373001

First Print Edition June 30, 2023

All rights reserved. No part of this book may be reproduced or used in any manner without written permission of the copyright owner. For more information email the author at: malcom@malcommassey.com

Book and cover design by Malcom Massey

Disclaimer

This book is a work of fiction. Names, characters, places and situations are the product of the author's imagination or are used factiously. Any resemblance to persons living or dead, to events, or to locales is entirely coincidental.

Acknowledgement

The names are too many, the reasons too numerous, but I wish to thank everyone who has encouraged me at any stage of my writing and publishing life. I wish you will find the encourager you need when and where you need it. My hope is for your greatest success to be yet ahead of you.

Siboney

Traditional Cuban Song of Unrequited Love

Siboney, I love you, I die for your love.
Siboney, in your mouth honey put its sweetness
Come here now that I love you,
and that all treasure is you, for me.

Siboney, to the cooing of the palm
I think of you, Siboney of my dreams,
if you do not hear the complaint of my voice
Siboney, if you don't come, I'll die of love.

Siboney of my dreams,
I look forward to you in my caney (cane hut)
Siboney, if you don't come, I'll die of love.
Hear the echo of my crystal(pure) song
Hear the echo of my crystal song.

Songwriters: Ernesto Lecuona, Jorge Omar Mlikota,
as performed by Connie Francis, October 1, 1960

*"The cave you fear to enter
may hold the treasure you seek."*

~Joseph Campbell

Table of Contents

Chapter 1	1
Chapter 2	9
Chapter 3	20
Chapter 4	28
Chapter 5	32
Chapter 6	46
Chapter 7	65
Chapter 8	80
Chapter 9	86
Chapter 10	98
Chapter 11	107
Chapter 12	114
Chapter 13	119
Chapter 14	146
Chapter 15	156
Chapter 16	176
Chapter 17	189
Chapter 18	198
Chapter 19	212
Chapter 20	228
Chapter 21	240
Chapter 22	251
Chapter 23	255
Addendum	i
About the Author	ii

Prologue

December 19, 1821

In the days when the Spanish pirate Captain Jose Gaspar became infamous, he amassed a great hoard of treasure. He hid this magnificent treasure at *Las Tumbas*, in a chain of natural limestone caverns lining the calm western bay of Scorpion Key, west of Cabo San Antonio in the far western extremes of the Spanish Province of Cuba. By doing so, Gaspar's goal of being as far as possible from the prying eyes of the Havana elite had been achieved.

Having unloaded his third Spanish gold shipment into their cavernous hideout in as many months, Gaspar called a holiday, permitting his crew extended leave and festivities for three days and nights, complete with courtesans imported from Colinas del Toro and Guantanamo in the far provinces of Cuba, rum from Jamaica, and pork from Venezuela.

The bonfires at their beachside lair lit up the sides and sails of the anchored *Floriblanca*, Gaspar's heavily armed vessel known to the English as the "White Flower". With the celebration now winding down on the midnight of its third day, the *Floriblanca* had been fully armed, stocked and made ready to sail. The following day Jose Gaspar and crew would make for the west coast of Florida, to lay off the coast near the growing port of Tampa Bay in wait of rich trade ships en route to New Orleans, Mexico, and California.

Gaspar leaned back, supported by scores of silk pillows in a grand silk hammock imported from Persia. Viewing the raucous scene, which at this late hour had devolved into drunken reenactments of opulent Spanish plays and dances, Gaspar watched with interest as men and women dressed for their roles from the plundered goods of the Dutch ships they had also overtaken and sunk. The musicians were drunk and off beat, but the Carib drummers kept perfect, rhythmic time.

Fashioned from a Persian tapestry hand-tied to reveal an opulent white lotus flower, Gaspar's hammock made a fine, throne-like bed once strung with new sisal rope from the Yucatan. There was easily room for two people, or three if properly arranged, and depending on their willingness to get to know each other. The hour was getting late. Gaspar surveyed the crowd for a suitable hammock partner to finish out the night.

Noticing that Gaspar was finally watching, Taina left the company of a dozen sweat-drenched female dancers, kneeling before the fire in Gaspar's full view. She swayed with tantalizing, planned movements. She knelt in front of him, reaching into the fire.

Gaspar enjoyed the view. Taina was his favorite, his Arawak princess, someone he had grown to appreciate and always looked forward to seeing.

Taina pushed aside her long black hair, then retrieved a skewer of savory bouccaneer pork and plum-sized potatoes from the fire. She twisted her light cotton skirt around the overheated skewer handle, as she worked to protect her hands. Taina turned to make sure Gaspar was still watching. She smiled at him, looking directly into his eyes before lowering hers.

Rising, the shapely Arawak woman sauntered toward Captain Gaspar, releasing her hair across her breasts as she gathered the last bottle of island rum from a nearby table.

Taina approached. The music faded. Time stood still. Beyond the crackling bonfire, the drumbeats became more intense, more insistent with her every step.

Reaching Gaspar's hammock, Taina twisted her unshod feet to plant them firmly in the sand, each gyration bringing her lower.

Gaspar sensed the steamy warmth of her body as she leaned forward, so pendulously close that the heat of hot bacon grease pricked his bare chest. Gaspar winced but made no effort to stop her. She handed him the rum bottle, holding back the skewer of food.

"*Y el tesoro, mon Capitan?*" the glowing woman inquired. "*Te lo suplico!*" She made clear her intention, her desire to know the answer.

Taina's eyes met his once again. Gaspar swigged back more rum. Taina had made no secret of wanting to know the location of Gaspar's treasure. She was well known for her determination to reach her goals. Gaspar was similarly determined to prolong the interrogation.

"Where is the treasure, my love?" she asked again, adopting a pouting face. *"I beg you to tell me!"*

"You will always be my only *tesoro,* Taina. I love you like no other woman. No other treasure holds value for me."

Having thereby declared his undying love, Gaspar leaned back expectantly in the hammock, considering the matter settled. Taina handed him the skewer of food, then stepped back, raising Gaspar's booted left foot high in the air, upending the pirate captain quite unceremoniously into the sand.

Gaspar somehow managed to avoid spilling the bottle of rum. The skewer of steaming food was not so fortunate. Two dogs immediately closed in, one snatching up the food, the other hot on the first dog's trail as they both ran away into the night. Their snarling echoed across the beach, out of view.

Gaspar stood up, brushed away sand, and leaned forward for a kiss, keeping one eye open. Taina smiled and stepped closer again. *"Certainly you can trust me.* Tell me your secrets."

"I told you, you ask too many questions."

"Captain Gaspar, I am your woman now. I deserve to know."

"My woman? A week ago, you were Pierre Lafitte's woman. Now you are mine? I will show you what you deserve. This is what it means to be my woman."

Grasping a handful of Taina's sleek black hair, Gaspar pulled her closer, bringing her onto the hammock with him. It was a pattern they had repeated multiple times over the last week.

Beneath the brilliant full moon and the shining stars, with a shield of long hair draping her face, Taina secretly smiled. She even pretended to struggle, to escape, mock protesting how rough and unrefined Gaspar was. Over this last week, many things had changed, considering the crew would be leaving soon, including that such impromptu relations between Taina and Gaspar had increased.

Taina knew that for Gaspar to have his way with her yet *again*, in such a public, uninhibited display, would secure her rightful claim as his common-law-wife. The Code declared it so, the right of claim of either party.

The edge of the fading firelight pulsed with human activity as other lovers coupled in the dark.

Taina submitted to his drunken kisses without revealing how completely she had tricked the mighty Captain Jose Gaspar. Soon, her future would be secure, her dreams fulfilled.

Unexpectedly they both tilted up and out of the hammock and onto the cool sand.

As he went over, Gaspar saw the feathery peak of a very pretentious admiral's hat. He jumped up, drew his sword, and walked around Taina, as she lay exposed and vulnerable in the sand. He smiled when he saw his old pirate comrade Pierre Lafitte, putting his sword away.

Taina knelt in the sand, pulling her hair back from her face as Gaspar reached for her. She stretched one hand up to Gaspar for assistance. At the same moment Gaspar reached for the upright rum bottle with his other hand. Gaspar was about to crack the thick, heavy bottle across Lafitte's skull when Taina intervened. She moved so close to Gaspar that no firelight passed between them. He could feel her heart pounding in her sweating bosom.

"But I *have* learned, do you not see?" Taina taunted, whispering directly into Gaspar's face. She bit his chin playfully, holding on long enough to get his attention. "I have learned that you desire me, that no man can take me away from you. I have learned to be a woman of peace, and that I will be your wife, that I will have your child, and therefore I will receive your inheritance."

Gaspar raised one eyebrow higher than the other as he raised the near-empty bottle.

"What about him? What about Lafitte?"

"I am done with him. He is no good, to me or anyone else. A different woman every night. I would not trust him if I were you."

"What else have you learned?"

"I have learned enough to know that I am also now your common-law-partner in the treasures you bring in. As such I will inherit your share of the treasure should anything happen to you, *Dios le protégé,* just as it is written in the Code of the Pyrate Brethren, as recorded by the *Pyrate Scrybe*," she declared, using soft tones as she stepped back. "And I will use that treasure to care for the poor, including your dear, abandoned mother in Havana, which is more than you can say, you ungrateful *cerdo*."

Taina covered up, bringing her hair demurely forward between her body and Gaspar's rough shirt. She stepped closer to him again, her breath steamy against his neck against the chill of the madrugada.

"The Pyrate Scrybe?" Gaspar enquired. "So you have been reading his papers, that stack of non-sense?"

"I can read, you know. The Spanish fathers taught me. In exchange, I helped them understand the Arawak culture, among other things."

"I'll bet you did," Gaspar leered. "But after our little "final fling", I'm having trouble knowing what a lady such as yourself, having read the writings of the *Pyrate Scrybe* as you state, sees in a scoundrel like me. Are you not discouraged with me? No gentleman treats a true lady thusly."

"Are you apologizing, Captain Gaspar? Because I'm taking your comments as an apology. My Captain, after what *'we'* just did, our little "fling" as you say, was not merely you taking advantage of me. I agree you are no gentleman, but I agreed to what we did, and I am now more determined than ever to make you mine and mine alone."

Gaspar stared, his mouth hanging open.

"You did exactly what I wanted you to do, perhaps a little rougher, perhaps a little longer, but *no importa*, the result is the same. Just like the four other "flings" you had with me in recent days. You have done exactly what I wanted you to do, no more, no less. Tonight the whole crew saw us in your hammock and now, I have witnesses to my claim as your common-law wife."

"*Manipulating wench*," Gaspar mumbled. "If you think this means anything, if YOU mean anything more to me than just another whor–"

Taina slapped Gaspar across his bearded face, smacking away the rum bottle while knocking the words from his mouth in a single well-aimed blow. The bottle spun in the air before rolling into the cooling sand.

Taina's eyes flared in the firelight. She drew herself to her full five-foot height as she moved even closer. Gaspar's face revealed that he had never been more scared by any man's pistol or blade. Maybe Lafitte had been right.

"I follow the Code, my *querido Capitan*," Taina threatened, wagging her finger in his face. "Remember the Code of the Pyrate Brethren. I have the books and parchments that belonged to the Pyrate Scrybe, God rest his soul. It's all written and recorded. I will be your wife. I will share in your spoils. I will bear your children, and if you double-cross me in anything, anything at all, I will cut your heart out and feed it to your crew."

Gaspar rubbed his chin, stepping back from Taina's warm, tempting skin and wide, crazy eyes.

"*Me entiendes?*" she inquired, a dove-like sweetness quietly taking over her voice.

"*Regreso en tres dias,*" Gaspar said. The girl held up 3 fingers, signifying her understanding.

"Three days."

"Voy a hacerle mi esposa en ceremonias civil y religiosos, para que todos sepan."

This time the girl's expression faded. These were Spanish words she did yet not understand. There were no similar words in Arawak or Taino.

"In three days, I will return. I intend to marry you in both civil and religious ceremonies," Gaspar repeated. "Now I must sleep for a few hours before my ship sails. Please go away. I cannot tear myself away from you."

"*Excelente, mi Capitan*," Taina said quietly. As she backed away, she blew him kisses and made other gestures of their love and friendship for him to carry into the dreamworld.

~The following account, from the warning letters added in to those of the Pyrate Scrybe, was written in a unique, childish hand, detailing Jose Gaspar's movements over his last days, based on ship's log entries and merchant reports. ~

December 20, 1821

The *Floriblanca*, known to be captained by Jose Gaspar and his pirate crew, sailed from Scorpion Key on the third of December, skirting the north Coast of Cuba. It then set a course north toward Tampa. The journey to Tampa would take five days, considering the prevailing wind and tides.

After raiding several merchant vessels, as well as those loaded with New World gold and jewels bound for Europe, the *Floriblanca* was sighted near the northern coast of the province of Cuba. The *USS Enterprise*, an American schooner assigned to piracy suppression in the West Indies, gave chase, leaving Havana harbor on December 20, 1821. The Enterprise caught up to the pirate ship early on December 21, approaching from the east just before dawn. Blinded by the low morning sun, the *Floriblanca* could not see the warship approaching. The *Enterprise* rammed the *Floriblanca*, nearly sinking her. A fierce firefight ensued, ringing the ears of those nearby with cannon, mortar and pistol shots that sounded above the tymphony of clashing swords and battle axes.

Swearing he would never be captured, a badly injured Jose Gaspar rode his anchor from the ruined deck of the *Floriblanca* down into the sea, where his crew eventually retrieved him onto his badly damaged vessel.

Jose Gaspar's crew had all been killed, to the last man. One wayward sailing captain, a raiding partner and a fierce pirate in his own right, rallied men from his ship to pilot the derelict *Floriblanca* back to Gaspar's hideout in Cuba. Pierre

Lafitte, Gaspar's former friend and romantic rival for Taina, had decided he could not beat Gaspar in any known competition, and so he arranged Gaspar's untimely demise. LaFitte even brought Gaspar's body back to Scorpion Key for a burial, wrapped in sailcloth and tied in ropes, appearing to have grieved the loss of his good friend Gaspar to the point of despair.

LaFitte then took Gaspar's treasure, buried it at the *Tumbas* Caves along the Western shore of Scorpion Key, keeping some of Gaspar's loot to woo Taina into beginning a new life with him.

Every *Tumbas* cave was named for the famous, or infamous person buried there. One of the largest seaside openings contained the Grotto of Gaspar. There LaFitte entombed Gaspar's body along with two thirds of Gaspar's treasure before ramming the *Floriblanca* under full sail into the mouth of Gaspar's Grotto, sealing it for generations to come.

No word has ever emerged about the location of Jose Gaspar's burial, nor that of his erstwhile friend Pierre Lafitte. Both traveled the same waters, loved the same women, fought the same enemies. And both suffered the same fate, having been lost to history, forever, or so it would seem.

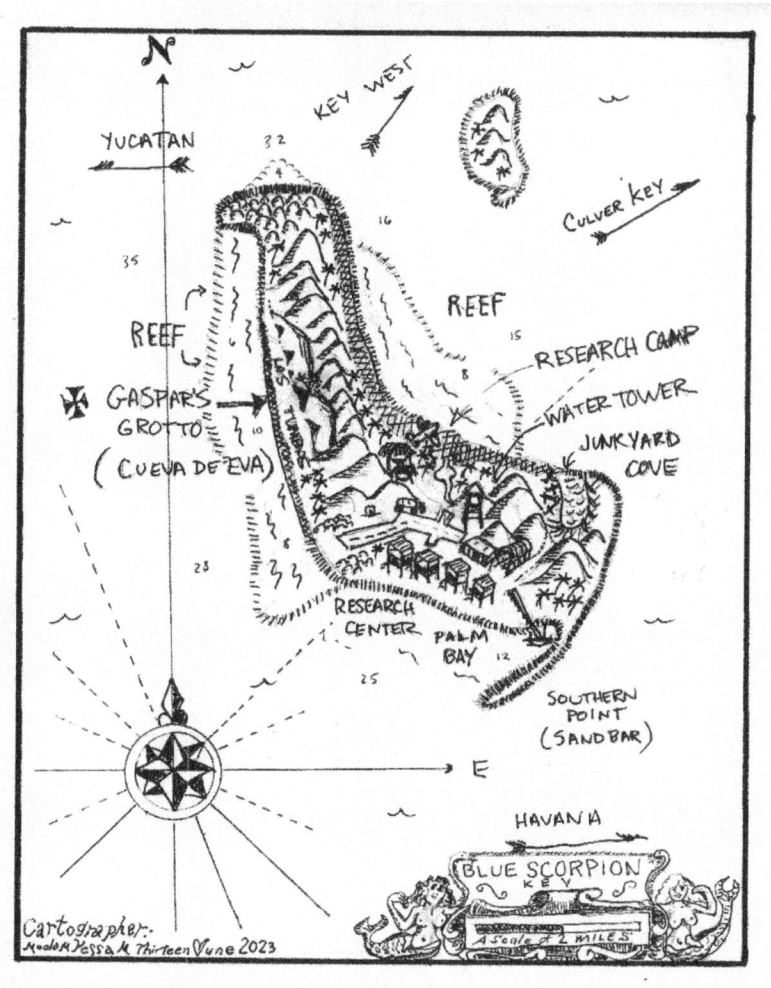

Chapter 1

Flight of the Albatross

Sensing a shift in the plane's direction, Sandra Culver looked up from the co-pilot seat of the ancient PBY Catalina to a cloudless blue sky. Nearly lulled to sleep by the twin engines' incessant droning, she listened as the propeller noise directly above her head dropped in volume.

The heat of the airless cockpit was overwhelming. Current airspeed in the lumbering plane prevented vent windows from being opened, to stabilize air pressure and to keep noise levels as low as possible.

"The Albatross", the nickname Sandra had chosen for the PBY, fit the vintage plane perfectly: heavy body, wide wingspan, clumsy ground movements unsteady in the air.

Turning away from the attacking glare surrounding the brilliant aluminum window frame, Sandra moved as far as the restrictive flight harness would allow, adjusting the heavy straps weighing on her back and shoulders. Her sleeveless tank top offered no protection against the rough canvas straps but given the heat of the cabin, she had briefly considered taking it off as well.

Blinding afternoon sunbeams streamed across her freckled shoulders, highlighting her sun-bleached curls before gathering in bright angular pools on the diamond plate steel floor of the pilot compartment. Sandra pulled nervous fingers through her hair, attempting to straighten it. Her shadow inched slowly across the deck toward Martin as the plane changed direction.

Glancing left, Sandra observed Martin sitting at full attention in the pilot's seat, but she made no attempt to communicate. His entire focus was centered on controlling the heavy plane. The last thing he needed was a distraction.

Sandra tried to focus on the positives.

They were finally headed toward their family, where Martin's father had taken their children for their safety to his Costa Rican hideaway. With any luck, in the next 48 hours she would see her children for the first time in nearly two years. A slight smile crossed Sandra's lips as she glanced toward the family picture that she had mounted near the co-pilot control, taken in happier times

Then there was the positive that Martin had survived their recent ordeal as he faced down their mortal enemy John Robert Chartwell in a literal firefight on Sandman Key. Chartwell was presumed dead after their loyal friend Fuse had destroyed the bridge of the LUN 903 that Chartwell had been piloting. If not for Fuse, Chartwell might have escaped, and although no one had found his body for positive identification, she felt that they were done with that tense chapter in their lives.

Sandra tried not to focus her thoughts on anything except reaching her family and helping Martin. Every other thought she entertained took her down a negative path. Her mind had been drifting that way since before the lightning strike that left her back scarred with a pattern resembling a surreal road map. Now the thoughts were more common, more difficult to escape.

Until just ten days ago Martin's sole flying experience had been limited to playing Flight Simulator games with their children. Since that time, he had learned to actually fly, trained by their good friend Dan. The plane belonged to Dan, another of his legendary vessel trades. Though badly burned over most of his body, Martin had toughed it out, completing the flight training in record time. Now they were finally on their way.

Martin's scorched brow glowed like a bad sunburn over his aviator sunglasses, his jaw and cheekbones set and tense beneath their thin wire rims. The muscles of his bandaged shoulder and arm, where they peeked out above and below the burn dressings, were visibly tense as he brought the heavy plane about to its new heading.

Like Sandra, Martin had shed his outer shirt hours earlier. As the temperature of the PBY cabin had risen, Martin had wisely advised that both of them take off their shirts, considering their position for this leg of their voyage, directly facing the sun.

Their long flight had been uneventful, save for their wobbly takeoff leaving Culver Key. That had been around 10:00am. It was now almost 4:00pm, and with no autopilot, no pilot breaks. The PBY was slow to begin with, and no longer capable of setting any speed records.

During those six hours, Sandra had thought a million thoughts, formed a thousand questions, and came to hundreds of conclusions. But she remained quiet, both a monumental exercise in self-control and in deference to the roar of the plane's thundering engines.

Martin clenched and unclenched his right hand, resting his bandaged left hand atop the pilot wheel of the plane. His left hand maintained contact with the controls as he flexed each aching finger.

Martin glanced over to Sandra, who signaled thumbs up with a questioning look on her face. Martin signaled thumbs down, then pointed to the deck, indicating their pre-agreed signal that he was planning to land soon.

Sandra nodded, confirming her agreement, then stretched to look through the forward windscreen. The glare diminished, but the nose of the plane was too high to see over. Unbuckling her flight harness, Sandra took a few tenuous steps, leaning heavily against the headrest of the pilot seat. Looking to the port side, Sandra could see a string of islands on the horizon extending along the shore.

Martin handed Sandra a small clipboard with a map of Cuba's coastline. A grease pencil line extended from Key West to the Western tip of Cuba. The numeral one was scrawled and circled at the end of the marked route. Day one's goal was *Isla Alacranes*. Scorpion Island, on the far western north coast of Cuba.

Sandra lightly patted Martin's back, feeling the tense quiver of his rock-hard shoulders, locked in a struggle with the plane's controls. Her intention was to reassure him that he was doing fine, but her touch had the reverse effect. Martin winced as if she had touched him with a hot iron. His sleeveless shirt felt damp, and when she pulled her hand away, her handprint could be clearly seen outlined in his sweat. His shirt was now stuck to the fragile skin of his burned shoulders. Standing this close, Sandra could see Martin sweating profusely around his neck and ears.

Returning to the co-pilot seat, Sandra buckled in just as

the nose of the plane began to angle down. Martin tapped the ancient liquid compass to release a random air bubble, turning his attention to their declining altitude. The altimeter alarm buzzed, indicating too rapid a descent, requiring immediate adjustments to the ailerons. Martin made slight, calculated corrections, urging the nose of the PBY Catalina up by scant degrees, just as Dan had trained him. Leveling off, he began their descent anew.

As Sandra watched, Martin returned both hands to the controls, gripping tightly in spite of his bandages. His blistered lips moved in silent recitation of proper landing protocols, or perhaps in silent prayer. Sandra did not know whether to feel grateful or afraid.

The white wave crests topping the turquoise waters of the Gulf of Mexico came into view, their reflection of the sun revealing a low, uniform chop that presented manageable prospects for a good landing. A steady westerly breeze occasionally rocked the plane as they got closer to the ground.

A large seabird soared into their path, darker and much larger than a common gull. It crossed the horizon directly in front of the plane as the PBY nosed down. Beyond the huge fowl, which Sandra guessed to be a frigate bird, four islands could be seen through the forward windscreen. The seabird remained on the periphery of her field of vision, nearly completely black with a forked tail. Appearing totally adrift on the tropical updrafts, the bird flew motionless, as if it were asleep.

A sudden gust of wind pushed the plane to the left, at the same time sending the seabird back into their flight path.

"Frigate bird!" Sandra shouted over the engine roar. "Two meters wide! That's as tall as you are Martin!"

Martin pulled back on the controls, nosing the plane up to avoid hitting the potential hazard, hoping it would glide beneath them.

The giant bird abruptly drifted closer, then appeared to wake up. Its now visible, red-rimmed eye widened in panic as it sought to escape certain collision with the plane. A showy red pouch inflated under the bird's neck, indicating the bird's fright at the plane looming toward it.

"Have to avoid hitting it!" Martin shouted. "Bad luck to kill a seabird, my dad always said. That old sea dog."

Martin reduced throttle and dropped windspeed as quickly as possible, hoping precious seconds would give the bird a chance to escape, but he was unable to avoid the imminent impact. The PBY was simply not agile enough.

The heavy bird slammed into the forward windscreen with a reverberating bang, a mangled slurry of blood and feathers sliding up across the cracked windscreen directly into the starboard propeller. Intense but brief shredding noise echoed from that engine as it stalled, its rpms reduced to near idle, having digested 2 dense kilos of bird flesh, feathers, and bones.

The plane lurched to port, its starboard side dipping dangerously toward the turquoise Caribbean Sea. In that moment, gravity became more of a concept than a reality.

Sandra felt herself rising as the co-pilot seat swiftly dropped from beneath her. The straps dug into her bare shoulders and chest as she floated upwards.

"Hold on!" Martin called out, unable to reach toward her.

"Martin, do something!" Sandra screamed. "We're going to crash!"

Chapter 2

Crisis at Culver Key

"Have you heard anything from Martin and Sandy?" Cita asked, appearing unannounced in the open garage doorway that led to the Culver Key boathouse.

Dan looked up from the worktable. He pulled an old towel across the coins he had been cleaning, not to hide them so much as to keep dust from gathering on his work.

"I have not," Dan replied, stretching his arms, "but I have not been upstairs to check the radio since your latest nap. What time is it, anyway?"

"I don't know, after 4:00pm I think. So, they are not supposed to do a radio check in for another hour yet," Cita said, rubbing her eyes, and her belly. "I just woke up and wondered if you had checked the radio. I worry so much about them. "

Dan pulled her closer, then hugged her from behind. He lightly patted her tummy.

"So how was your nap? Did you enjoy it?" he asked. "Did *both* of you enjoy it?"

"We did, thank you," Cita smiled. "I feel like I am sleeping too much lately, but I can't help it."

"You have never been a nap person," Dan said. "Not since I have known you."

"Except now that I am expecting this baby," Cita said, smiling. "I didn't feel like this with the first baby. I hope you don't think I'm lazy. There is so much to do here."

"Well, Samantha has been a big help, so far. She pulls her own weight, even does laundry, dishes, fishing. I thought I was the ace fisherman around here, but fish just seem to jump straight on her hook when she goes out."

"Well, that's good for all of us, and we need the protein, so I'm glad for that. Where is she now? I thought she might be out here helping you with the coins."

"Samantha? She went over to the guest house on the upstairs deck. 'Best time of day for sunning', she said, something like that."

"Aiiee! Can those Pirates motorcycle guys see her up there?" Cita asked, snapping her fingers back and forth. "That would not be good. She takes her top off every time. "

"No, I don't think they can see her up there. Now tomorrow, when they help me inspect the water tower, that is when they might get an eyeful, if she is out there."

"I'll talk to her. At least she has a place to herself," Cita remarked. "Without being here flitting around the house all the time, I mean. The guest house is perfect for her and gives us some privacy, too."

Dan pulled Cita closer. "Any more privacy and we would get in trouble," he said. "Again."

Cita pulled away. "You have caused enough trouble around here, Mister Dan," she laughed, rubbing her own exposed belly in a circular pattern. "No more trouble, please! I can't take it. I love you but now the baby comes first."

"It's not my fault," Dan laughed. "You were the one chasing me all over the island for the last 3 months." Dan ducked Cita's tiny, clenched fist as she reached to punch his arm.

"How long do you think they'll be gone?" Cita asked. Dan pulled her close, wrapping his arms around hers as they looked through the boathouse doors toward the Caribbean Sea.

"Martin and Sandy?" Dan inquired. "I would say a month, maybe less."

"They will be surprised at our news. Let's don't tell them on the radio. Let's wait to tell them when they come back."

"Okay, if that's what you want."

Cita gazed through the boat house to the ocean beyond.

"Dan, I'm wondering something. Why do you think they reacted like they did to the news about their son dying on the bridge in Norfolk?"

"How do you mean?" Dan asked.

"Sandra immediately cried, then spent all her time consoling me over the loss of our first baby. But Martin hardly showed any emotion at all. Did he say anything to you about it later?"

"No, Martin really doesn't open up like that."

The two of them rocked back and forth in the mounting afternoon breeze.

"I tried to get him to talk about it," Cita continued, "by talking about the loss of our baby, the day he and I went out scouting for resources and intact bridges."

"That was the same day you two found the Pirates motorcycle gang," Dan said.

"Well, I don't know if you would call them a gang, they're harmless. But yes, it was that same day. He seemed unaffected by the whole situation. Seemed strange."

"I think that is just an insight into Martin's personality. I remember when his mother died. We were teenagers. He kept his cool, kept things together, helped his Dad and his brother through it, even made the funeral arrangements. He doesn't process grief outwardly. Inside he was dying the whole time, just trying not to show it."

"There are some other things you don't know about Martin's relationship with the oldest son. They have had a strange relationship for years, since before the International Antiquities Foundation days. It always eats at Martin behind everything he does or says."

"What happened between them?" Cita asked, no longer rocking to and fro.

"The story I heard was that their oldest son expected Martin and Sandy to buy him everything under the sun once Martin started writing and selling novels. The kid wanted a fancy car, super-expensive college, all that. Martin and Sandra built & paid off a new house instead. They took care of their own future security, and that of their twins. The son had already moved out on his own when Martin and I were in Havana. Getting Martin to talk about it is like pulling teeth, though."

"I've noticed," Cita said quietly. "So sad. The only emotion Martin seems to show is that unquenchable intensity for Sandra, to love and protect her, to keep her happy and safe at all costs. That seems to make him happy. For him to take on this trip to find the twins and Martin's dad, I just know he did it for her. I don't think he was ready. His burns had not healed. He was not strong enough yet."

"You are right," Dan agreed. "Martin wasn't ready physically." He glanced through the garage to the boathouse, where the *Oro de Dios* was sitting on the boat lift straps. The large vessel sat level with the boathouse floor, the gangplank walkway ready to be removed for the treasure hunting vessel to be returned to the water. Dan had neatly patched and painted every bullet hole. The vessel was finally seaworthy again.

"But Sandra was ready. That seems to make the difference with him. If it helps Sandra feel better, he digs in and finds the core strength. I just wish he could have waited a few days and let me finish the *Oro de Dios* instead of taking that old Catalina. A PBY is a lot of plane to fly, even if you are healthy. Martin's got grit, I tell you that."

Dan grew pensive, then continued.

"Martin has been through a lot, Cita, more than you know. He has nearly died twice since he started chasing artifacts and antiquities smugglers. He always puts others' needs and concerns before his own. This time, with the pier fire at Sandman Key, and then back in Panama were both survival miracles for Martin. I don't know what keeps him going."

Cita thought for a minute. "He's like they say in Peru. *"Corre como una Toyota"*.

Dan looked at Cita's reflection in the oceanside window, where he stood hugging her. The sky had darkened several shades of gray. Now the sun was gone. With it darker outside than inside, their reflection became visible in the glass.

"I heard it from a guy in Lima," Cita continued.

" *'Corre como una Toyota'* " is their saying, kind of like when you say, 'Runs like a Swiss Watch.' Toyotas are known for dependability, so that's their example, like Swiss watches are known to be dependable."

"I always heard "takes a licking and keeps on ticking," Dan laughed.

"Who says that?" Cita smiled. "What is that about? Sounds a little nasty to me."

"I think it was a Timex watch commercial, not Swiss." Dan said, hugging her tighter. "You should go inside. It looks like it will rain soon."

"You better find someone else to bore with your silly commercial jingles, Mr. Dan," Cita said, extricating herself from his insistent grip. "And quit hugging me so much. Let me have this baby first, then we will have something to talk about."

Before Cita had taken a step, the clay tiles on the roof abruptly rattled with the rumble of engines. Dan watched the ceiling while reaching into the broom closet of the garage. He grabbed a shotgun, then watched a plane rapidly veer away, the sound quickly diminishing.

"You keep the shotgun here now?" Cita asked, rolling her eyes. "I was standing right next to that broom closet. You know how afraid I am of guns!"

"You said no guns in the house with the baby on the way," Dan replied, his eyes never leaving the ceiling. "I use it more out here than in there with everything that keeps happening. I guess you should know I have another one in the main house, up in the third-floor observation tower."

Now heavy footsteps could be heard on the roof, along with a rustling sound that was not palm branches. A balloon of parachute silk settled down across the seaward opening of the boathouse, trailing lines and an empty harness.

"Who goes there?" Dan shouted. Holding his finger to his lips, Dan silently pointed for Cita to board the *Oro de Dios* to hide aboard the dry-docked vessel.

"You know me, mon!" a booming voice replied from the roof. More heavy footsteps. Dan peered through the open boathouse door toward the main house. Before he had time to react, a booted figure wearing black tactical BDUs and a white tank top dropped from the roof overhang, turning a flip from the roof edge to the paving stones directly in front of where Dan stood.

"Fuse, goddamn it man, you should have called," Dan shouted,

"You should have paid your phone bill so I could have called," Fuse said. "Save your breath, you knew I was coming back."

Dan leaned the shotgun against the open boathouse door and gave Fuse a slap on the back. They both grinned. "You're right, I just never know when to expect you!"

"Where is Cita?" Fuse asked.

"I'm right here," Cita called from the open rear deck of the *Oro de Dios*. As she stepped onto the gangplank to return to the boathouse from to the garage, Dan rushed past Fuse to help her.

In that moment, in what would become without question the biggest mistake of his life, Dan knocked the shotgun free from its upright resting spot, sending the weapon into an agonizingly slow free fall to the boathouse floor. The barrel pointed directly toward Cita. She took a half step back, moving at an excruciating slow pace.

Slow motion ruled the moment. The next seconds were fateful, decisive. Dan immediately realized what he had done, all of it, the horrific reality, the impossibility of undoing his actions. He instinctively reached for the shotgun, diving to the floor to redirect the barrel.

Cita's face froze in terror, realizing her fate. Her eyes met Dan's, her hands dropping to protect her newly pregnant belly. Fuse leapt over Dan in his own attempt to deflect the barrel from pointing at either Dan or Cita. He almost succeeded.

The shotgun smacked the concrete floor, its barrel erupting in a shower of fire and steel shot that grazed Dan's left hand.

Fuse managed to connect with the wooden stock of the shotgun, batting it to one side before landing heavily atop Dan. But Fuse was too late also. Fate had spoken. The weapon had fired; the damage done.

Cita's eyes went wide as her upper body took the full brunt of the shotgun's discharge. From the waist up, her sundress shredded from a withering rain of steel, yet she did not scream. Her eyes rolled away, as if she was looking for an escape. Her open mouth made no sound in those final heartbreaking moments.

Two lifeless bodies fell at once, thudding heavily against the gunwale of the *Oro de Dios*. Cita slid slowly down to the deck as if she were sinking. In fact, Cita and her precious baby were already with the angels.

Dan tossed Fuse off of him as if the big man were a rag doll, jumping to his feet to run the several steps toward the *Oro de Dios*, his bleeding left hand tucked awkwardly but tightly under his right arm. His heartbroken wails were horrendous, his visceral misery fully vocal well before he reached the once beautiful bodies of the ones he loved most in this world.

Once Dan boarded the boat and saw the full carnage, he was inconsolable. He knelt beside Cita, gently kissing her shot-pocked forehead one last goodbye, her warm blood mixing with his on the newly painted deck.

Fuse stood to his feet. He did not curse. He gazed out across the dark ocean, the sunlight now fully obscured by clouds on the western horizon. Darkness descended and with it, the skies opened and rained down as if it were a flood of tears. Fuse knew there was nothing he could do. There was nothing anyone could do.

Had his eyes not been filled with water, Fuse might have seen a long, large sailing vessel moving offshore, making way at a respectable speed but with absolutely no sound. The vessel appeared to float along the surface without touching the waves.

A dark cloaked figure stood near the bow, with another figure, a much younger woman, holding a baby tightly in her arms.

The mysterious vessel sailed past Culver Key without a sound, on a westerly course, moving away at an unexplainably high rate of speed.

Chapter 3

Crash Landing

Lurching away from the shattered windscreen, Martin strained to see past the unforeseen obstacle presented by the frigate bird's collision with their plane.

Martin glanced to his right across the tilted cockpit. Sandra braced herself against the co-pilot seat, her face frozen in fear as she stared down into the turquoise sea only a thousand feet below her. The rough cargo straps were digging into her chest and shoulders, but she made no sound.

The right side of the plane had dropped precipitously below the horizon, her window revealing nothing but choppy blue water. Feeling Martin's gaze, Sandra looked desperately into his eyes.

"Let's get this flying brick levelled out," Martin said, his voice forceful, his expression grim. He assessed the situation instantly, though the scene repeatedly passed through his mind in extreme slow motion.

Trimming the left ailerons, he adjusted the right elevators to gain stability and altitude, then pulled back on the throttle. Roll tendency now mitigated, Martin felt gravity pull him back into the pilot seat as the plane's tail rotated past the center axis. Martin made slow, careful movements as he calculated the risk of going into a flat spin, having crashed too many aircraft in his life.

Sandra dropped back into the co-pilot seat, watching Martin's pinched lips morph into a stern smile as he struggled with the controls. The stern look soon took over his entire face, his eyes narrowing to mere slits and glaring like blazing coals brought to life, fanned by tension.

New vibrations and groaning metal erupted from all sides as the plane moved and reacted in ways not found in any aeronautics manual. Sandra felt her stomach making similar moves and noises in response.

"Not today!" Martin shouted in a deep, lower than normal voice. "Today we live!"

Hearing Martin's outburst, Sandra trembled as he began to laugh, a bit too maniacally she thought. She had heard that laugh only once, all too recently to shed the memory. It had been the night their team had put a stop to Chartwell's reign of terror.

Sandra remembered that same laugh echoing from beneath the blazing pier on Sandman Key as Martin battled for his survival. It was a response that declared, *"I'll decide when it's my time to go!"*

Surprised at her own clarity of thought in such desperate circumstances, Sandra fought down her whirling stomach and braced for the PBY to contact the surface of the water. Curiously, her life did not pass before her eyes.

Knowing Martin as well as she did after this long, Sandra knew his reactions to pain, both physical and mental. She also knew this was a critical time for him, for the both of them, their individual and family goals, their health or lack of it. A lot was riding on this flight. It seemed they could be in real trouble this time.

While the goal of reuniting their family was of the utmost importance and a top priority Sandra realized neither of them had been ready for this trip.

Recognizing that she was still not back to full strength following the lightning strike, Sandra was also starkly aware that Martin had taken on too much to attempt to this trip before healing from his injuries and burns. Their decisive but destructive final battle with Chartwell had taken its heavy toll, something not quickly recovered from. It was still too soon.

Martin began to curse as he laughed, which Sandra was genuinely surprised to hear. As a writer, a man of words more than war, Martin had long ago declared curse words to be a mark of ignorance. Martin had taught their children from an early age that cursing evidenced a vocabulary so limited as to be unable to offer a better word or phrase.

Now Martin cursed his luck, the PBY controls, finally cursing the obliterated bird. His laugh decreased in saneness as the seconds passed.

Sandra had watched him battle for their lives with every fiber of his being for close to half an hour, but strangely, Martin appeared to be enjoying the fight. Who or what Martin was battling at this point was not entirely clear, but his grim smile and tense jaw muscles revealed pure tension.

Thin wisps of smoke appeared in the cabin near the ceiling. The acrid smell of burning wiring ebbed and flowed, alternately stronger, then weaker. Immediately Martin seemed more alert, more focused.

Rallying with an audible shout, Martin regained full control of the heavy plane, reducing their current rate of descent as much as possible. He steered the plane into a wide circle, then shut down the fuses to the smoking control section involved, returning his attention to landing the plane.

Abruptly part of their cargo shifted in a harsh crosswind, sending the plane 45 degrees around, the tail outmost. Martin compensated for the unexpected spin by steering toward the perimeter of the circle before finally bringing the plane into a wide arc, fully controlled, corkscrewing gently toward the

Caribbean Sea that waited so inviting and peaceful 100 feet below.

Gingerly dabbing his blistered brow with his bandaged hand, Martin looked straight ahead. Sandra watched Martin continue to adjust the speed and angle of the plane, his jaw still set and tense. He sighted the beach through an opening in the offshore reef, aiming for the sandy stretch with less than 20 feet to the water.

Stiffening his arms, Martin brought the plane in as smooth and light as possible. Considering the PBY possessed the aerodynamic characteristics of a cinderblock, there was only so much he could do.

The V-shaped aluminum hull of the PBY smacked the wavetops as Martin worked to keep the nose of the big plane up. Creaking hull panels gave way to slight jetting leaks below the water line. Saltwater sprayed across the windscreen from their near-crash landing and from the still-spinning engine. Then the engine that had devoured the frigate bird sputtered and stalled.

Reaching to throttle the remaining engine back, Martin encountered the exact scenario he had been advised to avoid. His seared right arm cramped from gripping the controls, lurching to one side, pushing one throttle handle forward as he pulled the other back.

Responding to the loss of one engine and the pull of the other, the PBY spun across the surface of the shallow lagoon just when Martin had hoped the heavy craft had settled down for an uneventful short cruise to shore.

Revolving like a feather on a puddle, Martin and Sandra were both thrown to opposite sides of the plane by centrifugal force, remaining in their seats but dashed about like dolls in a child's toy.

The spinning seemed as if it would never stop. Sandra closed her eyes. That only made the effects if the rotation worse. She reopened her eyes to see a parade of palm trees that swayed high above the approaching shoreline. The majestic trees loomed large in the shattered front windscreen, their tall foliage passing by the ruined glass several times before the PBY finally spun to a stop, tail first and high on the sand, almost as if Martin had planned it that way.

He brought both engines to a low idle, adjusting the propeller speed on the left and right engines to their lowest setting before finally switching them both completely off.

Martin peeked over the nose of the PBY, looking out into the calm turquoise water. By entering this wide lagoon, the plane was now as safe as could be expected from sudden storms or waves. The tide was obviously on the rise, judging from breakers foaming across the coral bank leading into the lagoon. Nearer the shoreline, the waves in the lagoon were practically non-existent. When the tide receded in a few hours the PBY would be sitting higher and dryer, though first she had to be secured and anchored in place.

Martin unbuckled his flight harness, standing slowly to his feet, holding onto the back if the pilot and copilot seats for balance as he stretched his stiff limbs and joints.

"Nice landing, Mr. Pilot, sir," Sandra mused, standing to her feet. "Ever considered going into full-time pilot work?"

"I'm just glad we made it," Martin said, finally relaxing. His face showed strain behind the burns, but a smile was forming on his lips. "Not sure how well the PBY fared though. She's got a little damage here and there."

Sandra slipped on her shirt, hesitating to reply. "Like you said, we're here."

"First leg of the journey complete," he said hoarsely. Martin looked toward the port cargo door of the PBY, paying particular attention to the exit light above it.

"I knew you would get us here in one piece," Sandra smiled back. "Are you ready for a swim, or would you rather have food? What do you need?" she asked. "Martin? "

"Maybe just some rest. I have a hammock in here somewhere," he said without looking at her.

Sandra took a step toward Martin.

"I'd love to have a swim, then rest," Martin said. "I don't know about salt water on these burns, though. I wish I had a place to string a hammock."

Before Sandra could reply, Martin took one step toward the exit door, collapsing to the metal floor of the plane, smacking his forehead against the deck with a resounding clang.

Chapter 4

Say Your Prayers

"*Abuelo* Jack, do you think they will really come?" Enrique asked. "Will they come soon?"

Jack drew a ragged breath, but he suppressed the cough. This time.

"I think anything's possible, kid," Jack replied. "Every night I pray for their safety, and for ours. And I hope they do come soon."

"I pray for them too, *Abuelo* Jack. I prayed for my sister, too. Her fever is not better yet, is it?"

"No, not yet," Jack responded. "Sleeping in the front portico hammock will be cooler for her. I will go check on her now."

"*Abuelo* Jack, do you remember what my mom looks like?"

"Yes, Eri....err, Enrique, yes I do. Your mother has a beautiful face, and a kind smile. Her hair is beautiful when she lets it grow out. I imagine she might wear it shorter these days. Do you remember your mother's face?"

"Only a little," Enrique said, looking down. "But I'm

gonna see her soon and that will make up for the time we have missed. Tia Bonita says when you see someone after a long time, it's okay to cry a little for the time lost, then you get to laugh again."

"Tia Bonita is very wise," Jack replied. "I like Tia Bonita. She is very beautiful, too."

Jack's fingers unconsciously moved into position to hold a cigarette, if he had one to smoke. The tobacco he had planted was not mature, no flowers on the top, so he remained without smokes. It had been a long six months.

"You like her, *don't you*?" Enrique teased.

"Tia Bonita? No, I don't like her," Jack protested. "Well, ok, maybe a little, but only because she is good to you and your sister."

"And not because she has that smoking hot Latina body?" Enrique joked. He laughed and laid back on his pillow.

"How old are you? Where did you learn to talk like that?" Jack said, smiling. "I think it is your bedtime, young man. Now say your prayers and say goodnight. And don't talk about Tia Bonita like that."

"Goodnight, grandpa. I'll say my prayers after you turn off the light. It helps me to go to sleep."

"Okay, but don't forget anyone, especially your sister."

"Do sisters get sick more than brothers?"

"No," Jack said. "That is a misconception. Women live longer than men, in general."

"Is she going to die, Grandpa? You can tell me, I'm big enough to take it."

"No, your sister is not going to die," Jack said. "She will be fine tomorrow."

"Okay, Grandpa Jack, one more thing."

"Yes Eri…Enrique. What is it?"

"I know where two of your cigarettes are. I saved them for you. They are in the ceramic jar on the table by the window. The one with the lid."

"Well, thanks, Enrique. That means a lot. I am dying for one, in a manner of speaking."

"I wish you could quit, Grandpa. I'm worried about you."

"I wish I could quit too," Jack said slowly. "One day I will. I will try again, just for you, ok Enrique?"

"Thanks, Grandpa Jack. I love you. Good night."

"Goodnight, Enrique. You have turned out to be a fine young man. Your mom will be so proud of you."

"And my dad too, right? He'll be proud too, right?"

"Especially your dad, Enrique. He will be extra proud of how you have grown up. Good night."

Jack clicked off the dimming 12V lights he had rigged from scavenged automobile taillight bulbs. Tomorrow the solar charger would recharge the car battery he had rigged to extend lighted hours for his grandchildren. Unless it rained too much, which seemed to be every day recently. Civil electricity had been out for over six months.

As Jack walked onto the patio, placing the back of his soft, wrinkled hand against Elizabeth's forehead, the only part of her face not covered by the sheet.

She felt cooler, thank God. Perhaps Enrique's young, faithful prayers were already working. Enrique, the Spanish name his grandson had chosen for himself, was growing up to be a kind and caring brother. The 12-year old's new name reflected his growing identification with his adopted Costa Rica.

As he smoked one of the cigarettes Enrique had provided, Jack found himself hoping that his son and daughter-in-law would come soon, while there was still time.

Chapter 5

Recovery

Martin felt himself swaying, as if on a boat, slowly recognizing the feel of a gently moving hammock. The air felt as thick and hot as the sun-baked bandages on his hand.

Reaching up with his least blistered hand, he lifted the edge of something pliable and slick plastered to his forehead.

"I'm afraid to open my eyes," he said aloud. "What's this on my face?" Martin could see the brightness of the morning sun through his eyelids.

"Have I slept through the night? Where am I?" he thought.

"You're ok now. Go ahead and open them," a male voice quietly responded. "No one here to be afraid of."

"Who is this monotonous-voiced person talking to me?"

"Where is Sandra?" Martin inquired, finally looking around. The first thing he noticed were the beams of a loosely thatched roof. "Is Sandra ok?"

"She's been over at the pool I built by damming the stream with rocks, so perhaps she's bathing, judging by the amount of time she has been gone," the voice said. "Don't worry, the water is fresh, and amoeba-free. Our spring has a good flow, from those mainland mountains to the east. Good mineral content too. I tested it personally. And if she is bathing where I told her, there are plenty of bushes nearby for privacy. Not that there is anyone else here to see her."

Martin made no reply, trying to assess the risks in his situation. From where Martin lay in the hammock, everything looked upside down. He felt dizzy from trying to think, and from the pounding of his head.

"The banana peel on your face is for your burns. In addition, you struck your head when you fell. I gave you pain ointment to treat that bump, as well as your forehead blisters."

Martin blinked his eyes further open.

"How are you feeling?" The man had the voice of a clinician. "Mr. Martin Culver, is it?"

Martin opened his eyes wider. Turning to one side, he observed the angular face of a pale, younger man, sporting wire-rimmed glasses and a thin beard, sitting at a rough wooden table nearby. The young man's open shirt revealed a scorpion tattoo on his upper chest, alongside a necklace from which hung a bullet casing. His hair was longish and stringy. The scorpion was tattooed over what resembled a bar code.

"Have we met?" Martin asked.

Glancing at Martin, the man nonchalantly flicked a small

bluish scorpion from his worktable, then looked back to the open notebook that lay before him.

"Mr. Martin Culver, author, adventurer, philanthropist, Director of the International Antiquities Foundation. Martin, from *Martes*, the Roman god of War, Culver, from *cuphre*, Old English for dove. Your name literally means *"War and Peace."*

"Allow me to introduce myself. I am Neal, Mr. Martin Culver," the man said quietly. "Welcome to *Isla Alacranes Azules.*"

"Blue Scorpion Island," Martin inquired. "So we made it."

Martin tried to sit up, his voice echoing inside his head. "Neal, how do you know my name. How do you know so much about me?"

"I am aware of many…" Neal began.

"Hi, you're awake!" Sandra chimed, breezing into the thatched, open-walled cabin like a butterfly in a garden. Her hair was still dripping, her towel slipping. "You've met Neal, I take it?"

"Neal introduced himself. Sandra, what is going on? Did I crash the PBY? My memory is fuzzy."

"Best crash landing I ever heard," Neal said, giggling nervously. "Unfortunately, I didn't get to see it."

"It wasn't your best landing," Sandra replied, drying her

hair.

"I have only made *three* landings," Martin said in his driest monotone. "*None of them* were what you would call great."

"Well, this *was* your first without Dan coaching you," Sandra smiled. "You'll get better, I just know you will. But we have to make some repairs first. Broken window, remember?"

"Windscreen," Neal corrected.

" And the smoke, Remember? Anyway, Neal said there's a junkyard or something here. "

"But what happened?" Martin insisted. "Oh, that darn bird. I hit that bird. Yes, I remember. So what is this place?"

"Hold that thought," Sandra interrupted. "I'm catching a chill standing here: wet towel, shade, you understand."

Sandra disappeared beyond a thin, fluttering sheet that separated the sleeping quarters from the general-purpose area where Martin lay in the hammock. As she got dressed, her shapely outline could be clearly seen in the full morning sunlight. Martin was pleased to finally see Sandra filling out after losing so much weight. He was not pleased to see Neal watching Sandra's silhouette so intently.

"We made it to *Blue Scorpion Island*, which is also Neal's research station," Sandra replied from beyond the threadbare sheet. "Neal does scorpion venom research which has beneficial anti-cancer and pain-management properties."

"Does, performs, accomplishes," Neal clarified.

"Isn't that interesting Martin? Let me hang out these wet clothes," she said, ducking past them to go outside again, her hurriedly donned shorts and t-shirt revealing the excess moisture they absorbed from Sandra's body.

"The map legend I consulted noted this island was occupied," Martin said. "I assumed Cuban residents, perhaps fishermen, not researchers. Scorpion venom, you say?"

"Aaahhh nooooo!" Sandra screamed from nearby. Martin sat up quickly, too dizzy to assist. Neal slowly stood from his chair but did not go outside. Sandra came running into the hut, her t-shirt tattered by long, ragged cuts.

"Something was in the bushes!" she shouted. "I hung up the clothes, then I had to pee, but when I went into the bushes something jumped at me and tore my shirt! It snapped at me."

"Did you see what it was?" Neal asked in a matter-of-fact manner. He wore a look of mild amusement. "There are any number of possibilities to consider."

"Come here, let me see if you are cut anywhere," Martin said. "Turn around."

"I didn't see it," Sandra declared, turning her back to Martin. "But it clicked, garden-shear mechanical sounding, but quieter. Not a natural sound. It scurried up from behind me. I heard it in the undergrowth. Honestly Martin, I thought you were playing a joke on me. I was just past the ashy strip that runs around the camp."

"I am sorry for your fright," Neal said. "I am concerned for your safety. I am also sorry about your shirt. It is very revealing."

Sandra frowned, moving toward the changing area, grabbing Martin's t-shirt from the hammock.

"For now, I'm wearing this shirt, since mine is ruined. I am not going to the PBY for another one."

Martin turned to watch Sandra change shirts, outlined once again by the morning sunlight. He also watched Neal watching Sandra. When Neal realized that Martin saw him, he adjusted his glasses and averted his gaze.

"What do you think it was, Neal?" Martin inquired. "What are the most likely prospects?"

"The only logical choice, based on the data Sandra has provided, would be one of the larger scorpions on the island."

"How large?" Martin asked.

"I have documented one over two feet in length, mandible to tail stinger."

"Very interesting work you conduct here, Neal, but I don't talk about me like one of your experiments. With these kinds of risks, what makes it worth staying here?"

"I'm afraid it's really not very interesting work, Mrs. Sandra Culver," Neal responded. "One of the most boring assignments I have ever undertaken, although it may pay off eventually. The world needs new, natural antibiotics. Humans have become resistant to the petroleum-based medicines doctors have dished out over the last one hundred years. My motivation is to be the first to discover these."

Martin tried to interrupt, but Neal continued on, drone-like, as if he rehearsed these words over and over.

"Scorpion venom has powerful anesthetic properties, anti-cancer potential, even anti-tuberculosis properties that we hope to develop. Scorpions are known the world over and have been used medicinally since the time of the philosopher Plato. With over 1500 species of scorpions, it takes time to research all the variations. France leads in synthesizing the venom of *Rhopalurus junceus*, Cuba's rare blue scorpion, for cancer therapy, so they are our partners in a sense, or were before everything that has happened."

"Sounds promising," Sandra said. "Wish that had been around when my parents needed it."

"The trouble is," Neal continued undaunted, "Scorpion venom is expensive. Thousands of dollars for a gallon. My research involves the effort to identify the crucial ingredients in order to synthesize a substitute. I am trained to look for peptide chains, specifically. "

"I find that very interesting," Martin finally added. "Who funds your work?"

"Most recently, a grant from the University of Florida," Neal replied. "I have not heard from them in the last year, but as you know communication has come to a standstill. I could have a grant approved but I do not have access to grant funds out here in the islands. I have done research for UF in Virginia, Florida, Mexico, now here in Cuba. We operate in our own little corner of the world."

"I can see that," Martin said. "And I have seen very little of your place here."

"We have a full research laboratory on the other side of the island. The Cold War Era power source established by the Russians in the early 1960s still produces our power."

"Why not extend electricity to this side of the island?" Martin inquired, looking around the thatched hut to a myriad of battery lamps and propane lanterns."

"I am not an expert in that field," Neal said, speaking in a voice that could best be described as mechanical. "The human mind functions best at a distance from artificial electrical fields. I come here to conduct research in the most basic manner, that being direct observation and experimentation. Then I go to the laboratory to conduct my summary calculations."

Sandra glanced at Martin, who nodded in understanding of her meaning, giving her the go-ahead for a topic they had agreed to not discuss.

"Neal, we knew someone who had studied at the University of Florida, in Gainesville," Sandra said softly, combing out her damp, curly hair.

"Many people attend there," Neal replied angrily, not looking up. "Very few actually study."

Martin motioned for Sandra to change the subject, interjecting a new topic while touching his own numb face.

"Neal, what uses did you determine regarding the anesthetic properties of scorpion venom?"

"For major surgical use, it's promising for veterinary as well as human use. Anesthesiologists are always seeking new, side-effect-free anesthetics."

"I feel like I've had some kind of anesthetic," Martin joked. "I can hardly keep my eyes open."

"That is because you have received 5 cc's of the formula I personally refined. It is especially effective. You will receive another injection if the pain from your burns returns."

"Yeah, I don't know if I should take it anytime soon. I'd like to clear my head first."

"What other venom uses have you identified?" Sandra asked, following Martin's lead.

"Before the Night of Fire, the obesity crisis had gained international attention. WHO and UN Statistics tell us that by 2030 three-quarters of the global population is expected to be morbidly obese."

"We are learning so much from you."

"Thank you. I value my role as an educator. The connection to your question is that in smaller micro doses, this venom can also act as an appetite suppressant."

"Sounds promising."

"Neal, you mentioned your Virginia research. Virginia doesn't have scorpions, does it?"

"Just one, a very skittish small scorpion, great at hiding from people, the Southern Devil Scorpion. Not much venom, and not very potent venom at that. I actually took that research assignment to reconnect with the girl I met at University of Florida-Gainesville. I had just renewed contact with her when the Night of Fire ruined everything."

"What happened?" Sandra asked hesitantly, hoping her intuition was wrong. "Aren't you still together?"

"No, this person moved back to Britain before the Night of Fire," Neal said. "A work-study opportunity she could not pass up. I was to have visited her in London after she got settled. We both have moved on. Or at least I have. I think about her a lot though. She meant a lot to me."

Martin could hear the wheels turning in Sandra's mind.

"Neal, there is something that we should…tell you," Sandra said slowly, gulping her words.

Neal did not look up from his notebook. "I already know," he said quietly. "That you rescued Rebekah Jayne Osgood from Mexico after the 2012 Meteor Event? That you were acting as her temporary guardians? That you escorted her back to Britain? I know all of that."

Each statement that Neal made seemed to anger him more.

"Wait," Martin said. "You knew Rebekah?"

Neal's tone darkened. He looked truly perturbed. "Rebekah is the person I have been talking about," he said. "I knew who you were as soon as you arrived, from her pictures."

"What a coincidence!" Martin stated. "Truly a small world."

"Coincidence does not exist as a valid scientific concept," Neal said in a consoling tone. "Things happen. Statistical longshots do indeed occur. I can provide many…"

Sandra grew quiet., then spoke, placing her hand on Neal's shoulder.

"Neal I am so sorry. We did not intend to take her away

from you. We did not know she was involved with anyone."

"I am not offended by anything you have said or done," Neal said. "If anything, I am grateful to you. I understand Rebekah went through a terrible time in Mexico leading up to the 2012 Meteor Event. I was supposed to go with her to the Yucatan. Perhaps I could have helped prevent some of the misery she went through there. I chose to come here instead. Rebekah sent me many pictures from your time together. I went there to see her before she left for Britain. She wanted me to meet you when I came to Virginia."

"So you two were close," she managed to say, clearing her throat. "Very close, Neal?"

Neal did not reply, though his countenance changed.

Sandra thought to speak, then dropped her hand from Neal's shoulder, casting her eyes to the ground. Her expression revealed the truth that had just dawned on her.

"So you already know us," Martin said, attempting to redirect the conversation. "Incredible coincidence."

Neal removed his glasses, placing them on his now-closed notebook.

"Again, I do not believe in coincidence," he said. "The statistical probability of any situation can be calculated, if all the variables are known. I can cite many examples..."

Abruptly Neal stood, pinched his nose between his eyes,

then walked away. "Going for a recharge hike," he said simply as he exited the hut. "Emotions are so draining."

Sandra waited for Neal to move beyond the clearing surrounding the research hut.

"Okay so that did not go very well," Sandra quietly stated.

"He'll get over it." Martin replied. "Where did you sleep?"

"We both slept here. You slept better than I did. I had to keep checking on you and flicking scorpions off of you in the night."

Martin looked puzzled. "We both slept in this hammock?"

"Of course not, silly, there isn't room. There are two hammocks in the sleeping quarters of this little thatched hut. Research, sleeping, general purpose and kitchen. It's a very efficient layout."

"Two hammocks in the sleeping quarters," Martin repeated.

"No one was here. Neal left to go across the island. He had some late work to do for Eva, whoever that is. Another researcher, I think. I don't know when, or if Neal *ever* sleeps."

"Will you sleep here again tonight?" Martin asked.

"I'm hoping we can both sleep in the PBY," she replied. "No scorpions there, and we have the inflatable mattress."

"The heat and humidity inside the PBY may change our

minds," Martin said. "Could get very damp and drippy in there from our breath. But there should be advantages, like less bugs, if I can make it that far. Still feeling groggy."

"That's the medicine Neal gave you," Sandra said. "Makes you sleepy, he said."

Martin did not reply, then blurted out his thoughts as his eyes blinked closed.

"I do not trust Neal," Martin said softly. "Neal is not to be trusted. Call it a gut feeling for now."

"Oh Martin, don't start with your suspicions. He is ok."

"Neither is Eva," Martin whispered. "Don't trust her."

"Martin for gosh sakes, you haven't even met Eva yet."

"Mark…my…words," Martin managed to say before falling into a deep sleep.

Chapter 6

Revelations

"I was beginning to think this would be my last assignment, until you two arrived," Neal stated flatly, returning to his notebooks and microscope. He reappeared as quickly as he had left.

"Sorry about walking out like that. I'm better now. The combination of the pressure, plus thoughts of old losses collided. I find a quick hike results in a good, though temporary recharge. But it's going to rain soon. I avoid rain."

"I'm sorry Neal," Sandra said. "I'm sorry that Rebekah was taken away from you. There's something else about her we need to tell you."

"Perhaps Rebekah guided you my way," Neal said in an almost cheerful tone. "She is very spiritual, in the metaphysical sense. I do wish I could see her again. Perhaps I should maintain hope."

Martin made a gesture to Sandra to not reveal anything else about Rebekah to Neal.

"Perhaps at the right time, you will understand it," Sandra

advised.

"She wore her hair trimmed like yours the last time I saw her," Neal said softly.

Sandra blushed, running her hand through her hair. She considered if Neal had been the friend who dropped Rebekah off to the Martin family condo the night the Brit astronomer announced her move back to the UK.

"Why would this become your last assignment?" Martin asked. He raised his head while Sandy helped him sip the sweetest water he had ever tasted. "You're not giving up, I hope."

A peal of thunder rolled through the research camp, thumping with enough force to rattle lantern glass.

"Frankly, I considered that I might die here, with all that has happened," Neal said in a very matter-of-fact manner. "I calculated carefully, summed up logically, starting from when my supply boat did not arrive three months ago. I've seen most of what happened, at a distance, heard about some of it by Cuban radio. There is no internet to speak of after all that has happened. That's now a thing of the past, like all other communication methods."

"Why do you think that is?" Martin asked.

"Between the Night of Fire bombings and the lingering planetary impacts of the Meteor Storm on communications infrastructure, communications on a mass scale have collapsed. It may lead to complete collapse of society, as it has been known in recent human history."

"Have you been here the whole time all this has been going on?" Sandra asked.

"You might want to bring in your clothes from the line," Martin said. "The skies just got really dark."

"I will have to run," Sandra said in a small voice. "You know how I am about lightning."

"Yes, Sandra, you have exactly four minutes until it rains. In answer to your question, I have been on this island since before the global Night of Fire bombings. This island is like a ring-side seat on Armageddon, to coin an analogy. Always has been from the Age of Exploration, the Age of Discovery, the Colonial Era, right on up to the Post-Civilization phase we have entered now."

Neal continued without appearing to take a breath.

"I've seen all the recent events from right here. I watched New Orleans go up in smoke to the northwest, then Miami to the northeast. In fact, New Orleans is still burning, you can see the glow at night. The U.S. Strategic Fuel Depot at Lake Charles was a target is my calculation."

"So, you are here by yourself then? You and Eva, is it?"

"Eva is the lead researcher and the island caretaker

responsible to the Cuban government for what we do here. She has been here since the joint Russian-Cuban dolphin weaponization program dating back to the 1960s."

"Always the Russians," Martin griped.

"Is she your boss?" Sandra asked, breathlessly returning with her dry towels just as the rain began.

"I do what Eva requires, in exchange for being able to conduct my work here," Neal replied, "Whatever Eva requires, within reason of course. She tends *to think* she is my boss."

"What research is Eva conducting?"

"Eva's work involves solutions for the handicapped via humanoid robotics. She seeks solutions for human disabilities within the animal kingdom. To do this she has converted the abandoned dolphin facility, which at its peak held 60 bottlenose dolphins separated into individual tanks, to her own personal research lab. She is obsessed. But Blue Scorpion Key is Eva's show all the way."

"Back to *my research,* though, thanks for agreeing to be my guinea pig, Mr. Culver. Your invaluable assistance is appreciated."

"Research subject? I'm no Guinea pig," Martin objected.

Outside the hut, the bottom dropped out of threatening skies. Intense rain pounded the thatched roof, while gusty winds teased and lifted at its edges.

Curiously, Neal lifted his feet to a higher rung on the lab stool where he sat, without saying why.

"You are a guinea pig now," Sandra responded. "I agreed for you. Neal has created a pain-relieving infection fighter that will help you."

"I didn't agree to this. Why would I need another pain-reliever?"

"Let's conduct an update, shall we? Are you in any pain Mr. Culver?" Neal interrupted, notebook in hand. "From your recent burns, from any previous injuries, joint pain anywhere?"

Sitting up, Martin did a quick physical inventory.

"No, I'm not. I'm not in any pain." Martin stood to his feet.

"Good, are you feverish?" Neal asked, aiming a touchless thermometer at Martin's uninjured wrist. "Your extensive burns left you open to massive infection. Fever is the first indicator of infection."

"No, I don't feel like I have a fever. What did the thermometer read?"

"98 degrees Fahrenheit. Even."

"His normal temperature always runs low," Sandra remarked. "You were sweating in the plane, Martin. I was worried about you."

Martin stopped to think. "In my defense, it was about a million degrees in that cockpit," he joked.

"Impossible," Neal replied. "The surface of the sun is only…"

Sandra held up her hand to Neal. "He's kidding, Neal. Your scientific side is showing." She smiled, her lips thin and pale, her brows knit tightly as she observed Neal.

"So, it would appear that the venom extract is helping. Fighting your battles for you, in a sense. Considering the associated grogginess, be careful when you stand up."

"What about this banana peel? Is that part of my being a test subject also?"

"We can remove that now," Neal nervously laughed. "That treatment is also experimental, but it has anecdotal support. I'm attempting to relieve the potential of scarring on your most visible burns. Island people heal severely sun-burned lips with the inside of a banana peel. I added aloe and pitcher plant extract, which is also a pain-killer. That's the plant that stuns its victims before devouring them. I only used a small amount to test to see if you were allergic. Pitcher plants are prolific on this island."

"So, am I allergic? I guess not. I do feel the painkiller part. But no one is going to eat me, right Neal?"

Neal ignored Martin's attempt at humor."

"A small percentage of every population demographic is allergic to arachnid venoms," Neal stated, as if reciting from a textbook. "Oddly, these are not the same people whose systems overreact to bee or snake venom. So I was careful to use minimal amounts. I did not want to risk affecting your breathing."

"Well, thanks for that. You seem to have thought of everything."

As the rain continued to pour down, Martin watched Neal. The researcher seemed to be quite nervous, constantly watching and checking his feet.

"Everything except for a way out of here. Which brings me to a question. Are you willing to take on passengers when you leave?"

Sandra helped Martin as he moved hesitantly to a nearby chair.

"After all he's done for you, Martin, we should try to help him," Sandra pleaded. "How many passengers, Neal?"

"The truth is, Mr. Culver, I've run out of options," Neal said in a voice loud enough to overcome the pouring rain. "I will run out of some key supplies here soon, faster in fact since we are sharing with you two. I have the ability to fish, I have some fruit available, no coconuts though, despite many coconut palms. I have a decent solar electricity set-up here, a good raft in case of tidal wave or flood, good communications equipment, but no one to talk to. And I don't think my supply boat is coming from the mainland, ever again. I thought about rowing for the mainland on the life raft, but the currents are quite strong. That means we were stranded until the status quo changed. Until you fell out of the sky for example."

"I know exactly how that feels," Martin said. "I've been stranded before, on an island near Panama."

"Wait Neal, you said "we" a couple of times now," Sandra challenged. "You also asked about passengers in the plural. Did someone come here with you?"

"No," Neal responded flatly.

Martin looked at Sandra.

"But someone is here with you now, correct? Someone besides us?" Sandra persisted. "I need a specific answer, Neal. Yes or no."

"Yes," Neal replied. "Someone else is here now. You will meet her. I have mentioned her by name. Do you mind holding your questions? I'm trying to re-calibrate this microscope."

A bolt of lightning struck nearby, shaking the ground in its intensity. The smell of ozone mixed with the faint odor of smoldering fire. Looking frustrated, Neal started again.

Sandra glanced at Martin, a questioning look in her eyes.

"I don't mean to be rude," Neal said meekly, as if correcting his comments but without apology. "I would just like to finish this work. When I wrap up this assignment, I'm getting out of here, one way or another."

"You mean off the island?"

"Out of this shack for starters. Now I just have to wait for the rain to stop. But I do want to get off the island, yes."

"How long have you been here?"

"Too long," Neal laughed, appearing to suppress a dry cough.

"Do you have a boat or anything?"

"I don't have a boat. Yes, there was a boat, but it had developed issues, so it sank. It was basically just a spot to live. Eva has another boat. It's at a cove on the other side of the island that we call Palm Bay. Weird spot at the end of a long dock. That space belongs to the senior researcher, Eva, though. She wants it all for herself. I sleep here, when I sleep."

"Not a lot of room on any boat," Martin commented. "We understand. We're headed to Mexico. Will that help you?"

"Cuba is closer," Neal said. "My permits to work here were issued in Havana. I would rather go to Cuba, to…plug back into society is one way to say it. I am told my parents worked there for the Peace Corps, though I do not remember this myself. Perhaps I still know people in Cuba."

"We are only a 30-minute flight from populous areas of Cuba, Martin," Sandra mentioned. "Couldn't we take him there?"

"I think we can work it out," Martin agreed. "But I don't know how soon we can travel. I feel like I have no energy at all. I should probably eat something."

"Your blood sugar was very low when we got you off of your boat…err, plane. The medicine will help you rest."

"We just call it the PBY," Sandra said. "It's a flying boat."

"Catalina flying boat," Neal began. " PBY. Workhorse of World War II. Capable of water or *terra firma* landings. Fuel capacity…Watch your feet! Watch out for the scorpions!"

"Neal. Neal, are you all right?"

"Sorry Mrs. Sandra Culver. I am fine at the moment. Scorpions are coming out of the ground due to the heavy rain. Please keep your feet as high up as possible."

"Neal, there on the leg of your stool!"

Neal nonchalantly slid open a drawer, struck a flint striker and passed the tip of a handheld propane tank in front of it, lighting off a long blue flame with a certain popping sound. He leaned down, moved his feet from the stool rungs, and passed the flame up and down the legs of his seat. The few scorpions that dared climb were soon toasted to a crisp, smelling of burnt hair. He closed the gas valve with a pop.

"That was impressive," Martin said. "Now I know why you have been so distracted. You knew the scorpions were coming, correct?"

"It has happened before," Neal said. "It was only logical that it could happen again."

"Does it happen often?" Sandra said, shivering in fear.

"Only when it rains hard and lightning strikes nearby. The two things seem to happen in congress with each other, creating momentary havoc at the surface. No harm done."

Neal then changed subjects as if nothing had happened.

"Do you need anything to eat, Martin Mr. Culver? Do you feel hunger?"

"I *am* hungry," Martin said firmly. He stood up, leaning heavily on Sandra's arm as he watched the ground beneath the thatched roof.

"Sandra you are so strong now," Martin said. "Your arms are like cables."

"You think I am strong? Neal carried you here by himself yesterday."

"Neal, how far is the beach?" Martin asked. "From where we stand right now?"

"310 yards. 284 meters to be exact. How do you know

there is a beach nearby?" Neal asked.

Martin studied Neal, trying to determine if the researcher was joking.

"I'm just curious about… things," Neal said. "You were not coherent when we brought you here last night."

"I smell salt air, I hear seagulls, I hear waves crashing. The palms are leaning toward the sea. Your surfboard tells me something as well."

"Ah, the evidential approach. I too, prefer evidence to speculation. However, the surfboard is not mine. A mainland Cuban tried to escape north to Key West. Many of them end up here if the catch the wind or tides at the wrong time. "

"Where is that person now?" Martin asked.

"Gone, left, *se fue, se ha ido, ja no esta, "* Neal said.

Sandra interrupted, checking the ground around her feet.

"Martin, we could take Neal to Cuba, couldn't we? This seems like such a terrible place."

"We have the room," Martin agreed. "We certainly have the weight capacity. I feel certain we can help, provided we can get fuel."

"Then it's settled," Sandra said. "We will leave as soon as we get the plane fixed."

"Excellent," Neal replied. "I caught plenty of fish this morning. I will have those grilled up for you in no time, as soon as you check on your...the...PBY."

"That window will need to be replaced," Neal whispered, repeating himself. "There is a plane junkyard on the island."

"Why's that Neal? How did so many planes get here?"

"Neal is tired...needs a recharge...needs a walk."

Martin and Sandra traded questioning looks with each other.

"The boat you have here," Martin inquired. "Do you know what type it is? Sailboat? Motor launch? Does it have a name?"

"Please, one question at a time..."

"*Likely Story*," a female voice announced. "De *SV Likely Story*, hailing out of Key West." Her pronounced Caribbean lilt dragged out her vowels as it stilted her consonants. "My lovely vessel is a Marlow-Hunter, built in Alachua, Florida. Her keel was laid in 1997. She's 12 meters long, 4 meters wide."

Martin turned to see a dark-skinned, darker-haired woman in the doorway of the thatched research shack. She had appeared without any sound. The reason for that became readily apparent.

The woman rolled forward, strapped into a tall metal wheelchair with a high back, complete with silent electric motor and wide, soft tires that perhaps had come from a hand truck. Protective chrome bars hovered over her head like a race-car roll cage, gathering to a curved point with a hook and cable rigged for lifting.

Automated controls on the right side of the wheelchair fit between her extended index and thumb nails of her right hand. For some reason, she only had three very long digits, two fingers and a thumb.

The woman was trim, athletic, muscular. She wore several shell necklaces and a pair of black bicycle shorts. Her long, braided hair strategically covered her bare, ample chest. The skin around her eyes, covered in web-like wrinkles, was more than naturally black, emphasizing her staring, reddened eyes. The look on her face was nothing like a smile.

Her mouth had been modified with a split chin that closed horizontally when she pressed her upper jaw down.

A metal brace strapped across her shoulders carried the mechanical contraption that served to replace her missing left arm. That arm ended in a crude mechanical hand that had claws twice the length of normal fingers. Her legs, though shapely, were strapped together side by side, useless.

The sudden appearance of this new person unsettled Neal, while Sandra let out a surprised gasp, expressing both fear and surprise.

"Hello, Eva," Neal said in his monotone voice. "Have you

come to meet our guests so early in the day?"

"*I* have no need of meeting dese people," she said. "Dey are the ones who *need to meet me.* I am de only one who can help dem, with what dey want to know."

Neal winced, looking disappointed at her comment.

"Now Eva, don't start in with your stories," Neal taunted. "You must get out of the lab more often."

"How is that again, Eva?" Martin asked. "I must have not heard you correctly. What help do we need from you?"

"I can help you unnerstand de *island,*" Eva stated. "An important step to your survival. My family has lived here forever."

"Another likely story, Eva?" Neal teased.

"*Likely Story* is da name of my boat," the woman shot back. "I found her while roaming da shore after a storm a few years back. Rescued her, you might say. The owners were…beyond saving, God save their eternal souls. Neal knows the story. He wrote their last log entry."

Eva tipped her wheelchair back on the rear wheels, holding that position, then spun around once.

"Neal's boat sank last month. So sad that was. Mine is… less dan sea-wortty."

The rest of the group sat in stunned silence. Martin and Sandra were especially quiet, viewing the mechanical monstrosity before them.

"No one has anyting to say? I heard you talking about me before. Do I appear so strange to you? I call dis conveyance my "scart", my scorpion-cart. I have given so much to scorpions, but dey have taken so much more from me. I choose dis form, the form of the scorpion. It must be superior in some way. Dey keep surviving when da rest of us do not. In the future, humans will all be hybridized into insectoid machines, depending on our purpose and usefulness. Do you care to see my progress in dis regard?"

Eva leaned forward, her eyes staring, wide, questioning. Pushing aside thick, tangled braids, Eva pointed to the sensors embedded in her upper left arm and chest. The sensors had been crudely inserted, the flesh closed by someone less than a medical professional. The skin at the insertion sites moved, twitching and pulsing with each electrical signal that passed through them. Eva flexed her pectoral muscles, moving her chair left and right, swaying her bare breasts with each movement.

Martin heard Sandra stifle a retch. "We've seen enough," he said."

"One day, I hope these sensors will help me to walk again. Do you want to see the ones… down below?" Eva threw back her head and laughed an unholy deep laugh. "No, of course you don't."

Sandra left the tent, headed for the beach.

"I hate to break up this little funfest," the disturbing woman said in a low voice. "Neal, I've come for my share of the fish. With guests, I know you won't be back until late."

As she spoke, Eva raised and lowered her right hand in a smooth, ominous gesture. When she finished speaking, she snapped her fingers in conclusion. Her rings, as many as five per finger, clicked in time to her long fingernails that effectively had become claws.

Neal peered over his glasses at Martin.

"Excuse me, Mr. Martin Culver. I need to collect Eva's share of those fish I caught. I won't be long." Neal stood and walked outside with Eva.

Neal caught up to Eva's "scart". They began to communicate in a series of high-pitched clicks, whistles and whines. Their chatter was very animated, and each appeared to understand the other perfectly. Neal could be seen gesturing expansively as he walked beside Eva's vehicle. Then she stopped, looking angry, using her mechanical arm to practically shove Neal onto the small back platform of her "scart" before racing off up the hill.

Martin waited for Neal and Eva to move out of earshot. Sandra returned to the thatched hut as soon as she saw Eva leave.

"Did you hear that?" Sandra asked. "What was that chatter all about?"

"Weird. A more mismatched pair of people, I cannot recall meeting," Martin said. "And whatever is up with the dolphin chatter makes it even more weird. I felt like we were at SeaWorld as they were leaving.

"Agreed," Sandra commented. "I don' t know about those two. Did they learn that here? Neal seems the moth to Eva's devouring insect. I guess on research assignments you don't get your choice of research partners. But I don't like her at all. I hope for his sake they are not together."

"She's too old to be a college research student. I get the insect vibe you mentioned, but I define her mode as scorpion stinging prey for sure. Did you see her clicking those index and thumb nails?"

"I did, and truthfully, I don't like either one of them," Martin said. "I don't like any of this. I'm ready to leave. Help me take a few steps. I've got to build up my strength."

"That's the thing, Martin. You're not ready, to walk, to fix the plane, to do anything, much less to leave. Neal said so. You know it's true. Give it a day or two. We should have stayed at Culver Key a few more days to let you rest."

"Ok, I get that. Too late to reconsider leaving Culver Key,

though. We had to make this trip before hurricane season," Martin said.

"I know," Sandra commented. "And how many ships are there at the bottom of the ocean that said the same thing?"

"No doubt a bunch," Martin agreed. "I will find out where this junkyard is and go tomorrow for a plane windscreen."

"If you are strong enough," Sandra said.

"Agreed," Martin said. "First I need to eat."

"I brought back some of our food from the *Albatross.*"

"So, you've named the PBY? Is it growing on you?"

"Right now I hate it," Sandra admitted. "As much as the Ancient Mariner hated his."

"Wow, strong words coming from you," Martin replied.

"If it ends up being the best vessel to get us to Costa Rica, then I will take that back. Here, sit up to eat this," Sandra added, handing Martin a plate.

"Until then, we are stuck in Never-Neverland.

Chapter 7

Sandra's Discovery

"Do you think we can trust Neal now?" Sandra asked as she ate her lunch.

"I'm not sure," Martin replied between bites. "He is hard to read, so formal, so...robotic is the word I'm looking for. What worries me is that I don't think everything is normal here. I can't shake the feeling of entering a trap."

Sandra bit her lip as Martin ate, her face filling with concern.

"I wish there was something I could do," Sandra said.

"The only thing to do is keep your eyes open and help me back to good health. Then I'll fix the plane and we'll get out of here. Sounds like we have met everyone there is to meet, so there should be no new surprises."

"I hope you are right, Martin. Neal kept saying 'they' like there are many more like him. I feel so anxious. I need to relax."

"Help me up," Martin said. "I need to take another walk."

Sandra assisted Martin to his feet. "Where to this time?"

"Just around the shack, just 50 feet or so. That's all I can do. Each time I get up I'm going to take a few more steps."

Sandra guided Martin outside. He noted the wide clearance from the research shack to the undergrowth. A person could drive a truck around this building, Martin observed. The ground looked as if it had been burned with a flamethrower, and carried a slight smell of diesel fuel.

"Martin, what could these two possibly want from us?"

"Well, people pay big money for planes like ours. This plane could move a lot of cargo. The wrong kind of cargo, if you get my drift. We have to be careful who we trust."

"So we'll keep an eye on the PBY," Sandra said. "Trust no one. Plus we will be sleeping there."

"Yet," Martin said. "No one else is on this island *yet*. What's that thing you always say?"

"I know, I know. Trouble follows you wherever you go? The plane crash wasn't bad enough?"

"So we are due for trouble at any time," he said. "We've been here nearly 24 hours."

"I wish you would not talk so much gloom and doom, Martin."

"Sorry. It's how I stay motivated. What are your plans now?" Martin asked as Sandra helped him sit back in the hammock.

Sandra walked away, slipping around the sheet separating

the sleeping area. Martin could see Sandra changing into a two-piece bathing suit. Across her back, Martin's eyes traced the marks on her exposed skin from the lightning strike. These showed white against her tanned skin, like a reverse tree of life tattoo.

"I need to go for a walk," Sandra said. "I want to see what else is on this little island. I have the hand drawn map Neal left us. I can't just stay here and wait for Neal or worse yet Witchy-Poo to come back."

"Ok," Martin agreed. "I'm going to be right here. I don't have much of a choice. Watch out for snakes."

"And scorpions, the man said," Sandra smiled at her own retort.

"Scorpions, too," Martin agreed. "Is that what you're wearing to explore, a bikini?"

"Do you like it?" Sandra asked, striking a pose. "It's new, trendy. Cita gave it to me for this trip. Knowing her it's European."

"It's very revealing, that's for certain. Yes I like it. A bit cheeky perhaps? Don't get sunburned *there*. Take one of my t-shirts."

"Don't be silly, Martin. I have my sunhat. I'm taking diving fins Neal lent me. I hope to find a good pool for a swim. The water on this side is too choppy."

"It's from the wind," Martin replied. "Be careful, Sandra. Please be careful. And grab a t-shirt!"

"No worries, Martin, I will. Now get some rest. Neal should be back soon, so pretend to be asleep. Maybe he'll be quiet. I'll be gone an hour or two. Maybe I'll find something cool, a *recuerdo* of our short time here."

Sandra blew Martin a kiss and departed the camp, picking up a walking stick as she left, stuffing her ripped t-shirt into the backpack. She felt Martin's eyes watching her, enjoying that he still paid her that kind of attention.

Heading north along the beach, Sandra established an easy pace and soon rounded the rocky northern cape. The rocks were wet and slick. She gazed across the blue water, trying to see Key West before turning toward the less hostile western shoreline of the island.

Soon the rocks gave way to wide sand-covered beaches cut by occasional shallow rivers. In the far distance, Sandra could make out a single tiny white sailboat in the mouth of a shallow bay, moored at the end of a very long dock.

Sandra had not walked a full mile past the rocks when she looked west, toward the coastal mountains that separated this beach from Neal's camp. She nearly gasped at the beauty of the view. With the tide at its lowest point, open-mouthed caves could be seen, including one cave with a higher, darker entrance.

A crystal-clear river of unknown depth flowed out of the largest cave, the water glinting golden in the sunlight. Cream-colored sand dunes mounded high in rounded heaps on either side of the main cave opening, while just above, a dense thicket of bushes, short palms and underbrush grew, interspersed with a few taller palms. The elements combined to give the appearance of a woman lying on her back, knees spread apart. Mother nature, ever the artist, doing a self-portrait, Sandra mused.

Something possessed Sandra to explore the largest, primary cave first. She immediately turned away from the sea to walk toward it, as if magnetically drawn. Though not at the center of the multiple dark caves she observed, this certain cave had the highest opening. Presumably it would be the easiest to explore, with more natural light.

Why she felt attracted to this particular cave, Sandra could not explain, only that it seemed familiar to her, as if she had seen it before. She checked her watch. An hour had passed since she left the camp. Noting the time as extreme low tide, Sandra then walked toward the cave opening, determined to explore it before the tide returned. She decided to return to the beach in one hour, giving her one more hour of travel back to camp before the sun would start to set.

As Sandra neared the cool shade of the cave mouth, still walking on coarse sand, she stopped to probe the water's depth as well as the bed of the stream flowing from the cave. Initial probes revealed the stream bed to be stable. Sandra pushed the walking stick further into the sand, then pulled it out quickly, creating a gasping, sucking sound. Thick clay lay beneath the sand.

Freeing the walking stick, Sandra was surprised to see two gold coins glinting in the stream. She hurriedly reached into the clear water to pick them both up, nearly losing one swimming fin from the net backpack she had borrowed in the fast-moving water.

The first coin was dated 1717 and was in near perfect condition. It was a gold Spanish escudo, engraved with a Spanish cross from the reign of King Felipe V. From their experiences with Jeff Lyons after finding old coins in the Florida Keys, Sandra knew this coin was a two escudo, therefore a doubloon, most likely minted in Bogota, Colombia. The second coin was harder to read, having suffered more scouring by sand, its image and date nearly worn away, but it was still brilliant and shiny, as gold should be. No more coins surfaced as she probed further.

Intrigued, Sandra tucked the coins into her bikini top, stepped into the stream and entered the cave, her heart beating faster. Swiftly flowing water moved past her ankles, her knees, then finally rose to her waist. She began to have second thoughts, waiting for her eyes to adjust from the brightness of the day to the dim interior of the cave. Sandra continued forward, against the flow.

Entering the shade of the overhanging cave, Sandra's expectations were met when the fast-moving water immediately grew colder. She soon felt the coldest water she had encountered yet, from her waist down. A shiver ran through her as she considered what the source of the cold, fresh water might be. Dressed for a sunny beach, Sandra reconsidered her wardrobe choices for exploring this cavern. Martin had been right about the t-shirt, though he was thinking sun protection. Good thing she grabbed one on the way out.

The allure of gold was strong. Perhaps there would even be pirate gold. Sandra felt her heart racing.

Pausing to let her eyes adjust, Sandra noticed a beam of bright sunlight entering the cave at a steep angle. She looked up to see the sky through a wide circular gap in the top of the cavernous space. The midday sun streamed in, adequately lighting the flowing stream, revealing a small, sandy beach nestled between low, rocky outcrops. The beach looked to be just wide enough for two people to relax in the sun in peace, quiet and complete privacy. The rest of the cave floor looked rocky, slick and wet.

Lifting her backpack high above her sun hat, Sandra made her way to the sunny mini-beach. The water resisted her efforts, rising to her navel, then higher, flowing out toward the sea at a brisk pace. Reaching the tiny shoreline, Sandra waded out of the cool water, stepping ashore dripping wet. She remembered she had neglected to bring a towel at the same moment she realized she was covered with chill-bumps. She had not waded deep enough to wet her turquoise bathing suit top, but her tiny black bottoms delivered a sudden, intense chill in the steady breeze that passed through the cave.

Sandra moved into the pool of warming sunlight, placing her backpack on the sandy beach, then firmly planting the walking stick vertical in the sand.

Glancing around to confirm she was alone, Sandra dropped her damp bathing suit bottoms, hanging them to dry on the upright stick.

At second thought, she slipped out of her bikini top too, so that it would not get wet as she explored and perhaps chill her even further. Martin's idea of a cover up t-shirt was just what the doctor ordered, but she had chosen the ripped one, one of her shortest T's that barely reached her hips. Still, it was warmer than anything else she had brought.

Retaining the woven sunhat, Sandra removed its long scarf at headband to string around her hips like a thin, low sarong, a makeshift coverup at best. With enough length to encompass her small waist, had the scarf been wider, it might have provided better coverage.

Though it was still early in the afternoon, Sandra realized she could not delay when there was so much of this cave to explore. Rather than walk to the darkest corners, she began by walking away from the sea toward a high-domed chamber that was best lit by the available light. The smooth rock of the cave floor was easy on her bare feet, as long as she was careful to not slip.

If Martin could only see her now, Sandra thought. She commended herself for letting down her hair enough to explore in her current state of undress. She also wondered where she would carry anything she might find, were there indeed treasures to be found.

It was then that she thought about the gold coins. She had inadvertently let them drop to the sand when she removed her bikini top. She would have time, she convinced herself, to retrieve them on the way out.

Reaching the highest point of the cave floor, Sandra turned to see the patch of sunlight moving away from the tiny beach. From this vantage point, she would also see any inflow of seawater into the cave. Perhaps the tide had turned. She knew her time for exploration was limited.

Moving along the diminishing cave opening, where the ceiling became dramatically lower, Sandra reached the rear wall furthest from the sea before she ran out of light. Curiously, a shallow squared-off shelf greeted her, obviously man-made, about two meters wide by three meters high. The shelf was less than a half meter deep, and held nothing more interesting than a pile of old sail cloth, or so it seemed. Other than a few twigs, straw and pieces of seaglass, nothing remarkable stood out. It resembled an altar.

Poking the sailcloth packet with one finger, Sandra commended herself again, this time for her good judgement in not reaching out to grasp the cloth bundle. Two rats ran out of the pile, one in each direction, more scared of her than she was of them, if that were possible. The rats shrieked louder than any noise Sandra was capable of.

When she stopped screaming, Sandra poked at the sailcloth bundle again. This time nothing ran out, but Sandra marveled at how solid the bundle felt, not like metal or even wood. Reaching up, she slid the dusty bundle toward herself, careful not to breathe the dust. She was also careful not to disturb the rest of the nest materials. True packrats, no doubt escaped from some past shipwreck.

The outer bundle was indeed tattered sailcloth, but surprisingly intact as she peeled back these initial layers. Soon, a good quality oil cloth revealed itself, neatly folded and tied with leather bands. What was inside could only be guessed, but the general shape and weight indicated a possible book or set of books. Now Sandra's heart really began to beat faster.

If Martin's thing was ancient artifacts and the countries they rightfully belonged to, Sandra's passion was the research, the background material, the proof. Her hands literally shook as she held the bundle, imagining what information it might possibly contain.

Reigning in her imagination, Sandra noticed the light in the cave had dimmed considerably. She turned away from the cave shelf, looked back toward the mini-beach, and uttered a rare curse.

In the short time Sandra had been focused on the shelf and the bundle, the tide had risen significantly, entering the cave to the point of half-obscuring the main opening. Her belongings were in danger of being swept away, including her bathing suit and the borrowed diving fins. Sandra had a sudden picture of herself waltzing down the beach back to camp without her bathing suit...the sun hat was big, but not that big. Her t-shirt and scarf-sarong covered hardly anything.

Hurrying down the slippery rock surface toward the upright walking stick, Sandra rushed a little too fast, slipping down to the rocky surface with a loud smack, landing squarely on her upper thighs. Jumping up immediately, she tried not to think how bad the bruises would be, instead considering how she would safely transport the fragile oil cloth bundle. There was no time to open the oil cloth or assess its contents. Sandra simply had no time to lose. For a half-second, she considered replacing the bundle on the shelf, but the risk of rats chewing on it was too real.

Nearly naked and chilled to the bone, Sandra felt as if she were freezing. Without direct sunlight, given the insistent breeze blowing even stronger through the cavern, every part of her from scalp to toes tensed and strained, craving an unfound warmth. Since the lightning strike, she had found herself to be so much less tolerant of cold.

As the incoming tide lapped at her feet, Sandra grabbed her bathing suit from the walking stick, then jumped back in fright. A huge scorpion reared its tail, perched on the very top of the upright stick. At least ten inches in overall length, the aggressive arachnid slowly flexed its claws at Sandra. Its legs and tail were blue, the fat body a reddish hue.

With her hands full, Sandra placed the oil cloth bundle on the rock outcropping near her backpack, above the swirling sea water. After inspecting and wiggling into her damp bikini bottoms, Sandra pulled the elastic top back like a giant rubber band, aiming for and then snapping it at the scorpion, cleanly knocking the giant insect off the walking stick on the first try. The scorpion landed on some nearby rocks, then slipped between two of them to hide. The water had risen nearly to her knees by this time.

Sandra closely inspected her bathing suit top for unwelcome visitors, then slipped it on, quickly calculating that the water she would have to pass through to be least chest deep by now, perhaps higher. To make matters worse, sea water now flowed in freely, threatening to trap her inside the cave. As the other entrances became closed by the sea, warm seawater mixed with cool rocks, and the cavern soon filled with a salty, foggy mist that stung her eyes and made everything slick, further limiting available light.

Thinking fast, Sandra grabbed the backpack from the nearby rock shelf, emptied it carefully and slipped the diving fins onto her feet, but not before a flashlight on a lanyard rolled free, having been tucked into one of the fins.

Diving fins, longer and more flexible than simple swim fins, were also much more floppy and awkward on land. The fit was a little loose, but a quick adjustment took out most of the wiggle.

The oil-cloth bundle was a perfect fit for the net backpack. Sandra whipped off her straw hat, inserted the oil cloth bundle into it, then wrapped the package in her t-shirt before tucking everything into the backpack. Using the scarf-sarong, she tightly tied the backpack to one end of the walking stick.

With rising foamy water now up to her shivering thighs, Sandra doubled the backpack straps around the walking stick, holding it high over her head to test their combined strength. The bundle, at perhaps only a kilo of weight, seemed so much heavier at the end of her walking stick. She knew that keeping the bundle as dry as possible was her best move.

The highest opening to the cave was now nearly covered by intruding seawater. Sandra slipped the flashlight lanyard over her head and turned it on, flashing the surprisingly strong beam of the light around the cavern. The floor and walls literally crawled with scorpions evading the rising sea.

At that moment the sound of creaking wooden planks began to move and rattle in the darkness to Sandra's left. She glanced up to see the partially sunken bow of a wooden ship swirling between herself and the cave entrance, complete with carved wood resembling so many exotic white flowers. The smell of rotting wood was intense and foul. Where the ship had come from was anyone's guess. All she knew at the moment was that it stood between herself and her freedom.

"A ship, inside a cave? Really?" Sandra shouted, shaking one fist at no one in particular. She held the backpack bundle tightly, awkwardly backing into the cold, foamy sea water.

Sandra stepped away from the beach into swirling water, backpack held high above her head. Sandra tucked the walking stick inside her bathing suit top and the waistband of her bottoms, holding it as close as possible for maximum stability, using one hand to swim and guide herself forward. Unable to touch the bottom, Sandra kicked her fins, treading water as she made her way toward the cave entrance. There was now less than one foot between wavetops and the highest point of the cave entrance. Daylight was slipping away.

High above, a horrifying figure at the edge of the opening in the cave ceiling observed Sandra's struggles silently, then shook its dread-locked head side to side. Rhythmically clicking extended index and thumb nails together on one hand, a sour expression crossed what appeared to be an insect's lower mandible.

There was no reason to watch further. Things had taken a turn. Spinning on invisible heels, the shapeless figure whirred smoothly away, appearing to glide over the rocky surface, across the nearby tarmac and into the dense tropical forest.

Chapter 8

A Somber Occasion

At sunset the following day, two exhausted men finished the somber task of shoveling sand and dirt back onto the graves of Cita Tate and her unborn child. Together they stood, brushing dirt from their clothing before paying their last respects. Fuse brushed his cheek with the back of his broad hand, then turned back to Dan. Neither of them had spoken for hours. They had done what they needed to do.

Dan spoke first.

"No word from the Pirates?" Dan asked. "One was a chaplain, right?"

"Nope, no word. Off hunting motorcycle parts and gasoline. I know they are good fishermen. Not much else. Some of these cross-key canals have great fishing when the tide changes. That's probably where they are."

"And Samantha?" Dan asked. "Any word at all today?"

"None," Fuse replied. "I think she's gone, location unknown. Probably couldn't take the idea of another funeral here. Or she could just be scavenging on the other keys."

"This little cemetery is getting crowded," Dan remarked,

wiping sweat from his face with the dirt-streaked bandages Fuse had applied to his hand. "I still have to clean up the carpentry shop and the *Oro de Dios*. Thanks for helping me pull the teak off that derelict boat for proper caskets."

Picking up a half-empty bottle of rum from the soft ground with his good hand, Dan took three full swallows before gasping for air.

"I'm leaving," Dan announced. He scanned Fuse's dark face for a clue as to his response. "I have to leave this place. I can't stay here."

"It wasn't your fault," Fuse reminded him. "Go easier on yourself, mon."

"Then whose fault was it?" Dan exploded in drunken exasperation. "It wasn't your fault, it wasn't my fault, but my wife and baby are *dead*. It was my fault, it is my fault, going all the way back to leading a late-season fishing charter with minimal supplies in the face of storm warnings. Before that everyone was happy. Everything was great."

"You had not even met Cita, then, Dan."

"I almost wish I had never known her. To lose her now hurts worse than if she was never here at all."

"Dan, listen..."

"Fuse, I don't even know if I had a boy or girl, only that they are gone, they're both gone, counting Cita, too. No hospital to call, no helicopter to help, nothing. I can't stand it."

"A hospital could not have helped them, Dan. It happened too fast man. Dese tings happen. You can't change it. What is going on with you? Keep it together."

"Fuse, I can't live with myself. I know how to handle a shotgun. I know better than to let this happen. I've got more shells. Maybe I should just join my family and save myself and everyone else a lot of trouble, because these next few weeks are not going to be pretty, I'm telling you."

"Why do you talk that way, Dan? It was an accident, mon. Look at my arms. These burn scars were no one's fault, not mine, not anyone. It was *the accident's fault*. No one wanted this to happen." Fuse paused. "I locked up all the guns, to be safe."

"Safe," Dan said, dropping to his knees at the foot of the twin graves. He screamed for the longest time, letting all the remaining anguish out.

"I would have done anything, given everything to protect them, to have them be alive and well. I would trade places with them right this minute if I could. I pulled her out of the hell that the mainland has become. We were starting over. Why did this have to happen??"

"Neither of us can answer that," Fuse counseled. "With

time, we understand these things. You will understand one day. Just not today."

"Oh yeah, well why were you up on the fricking roof anyway?" Dan asked accusingly. "You never have explained that one." Now the rum was talking.

"I did tell you before, Dan. It just doesn't register when you are in drunken denial mode. I get that. So here it is again. I got a ride back from the islands with a pilot I know we can trust. He saw the thunderstorm rolling in, and knew he had no time to land and take off again. He had a parachute, so I took it and jumped. It really is as simple as that. The rising storm wind blew me off course, so instead of the beach side, I ended up on the boathouse roof. I did not mean for this to happen."

Dan took another swig from the near-empty Cruzan rum bottle. He did not gasp this time.

"I know what you're saying is true, Fuse. I just cannot accept it, that's all. I was holding Cita in my arms one minute, alive and well. We had our whole lives in front of us. The next minute she was gone. Just like that, no warning. It really is more than I can take. Things shouldn't be this way."

"Dan, this is exactly how things *have to be*. It's how life goes. It's what makes life precious. You never know how much time you have."

Dan reached his uninjured hand to Fuse. "Help me up," he said in a quiet voice. Fuse pulled Dan to his feet.

"The sun is settin' Dan. Let me say some words," Fuse said, pulling off his do rag. "This will make it better."

What Fuse was really thinking was neither of them had a torch. He wanted to go back to the house while Dan could still walk.

"Okay," Dan said, leaning heavily on his shovel.

"The Lord is my Shepherd..." Fuse began. "I shall not want."

"Wait, they say that at every funeral," Dan said. "Isn't there something better?"

"No Dan, dere's nuttin' better. Dese words work is why dey say them. This will carry them safe into God's arms. You should listen to it closely, too. The Good Shepherd never loses a single lamb. Now may I?"

"Sure man, I'm sorry, I'm just a little, you know..." Dan's face and lips curled up like a baby. Then he began to cry again. "You know..." he repeated. "I can't say it out loud."

"Trust me, I know, mon," Fuse said. "I been dere myself."

Fuse reached out and put his arm around Dan's shoulder, steadying the crushed widower as he finished quoting the 23rd Psalm. In the fading sunlight, Fuse handed Dan two bundles of flowers he had collected from around the estate. Dan carefully laid the flowers on the side-by-side graves, one larger, one smaller.

Dan finally managed to say goodbye. Together the two men walked back to the main house as the sun dipped into the sea, with Fuse finishing off the bottle of rum, to keep Dan from drinking it, as much as anything else.

"I'm still leaving this place," Dan said, weaving his way to the house. "I'm going away. I'm going to make things better, you'll see. I'll fix things up just right."

Chapter 9

Missing in Action

Still feeling groggy, Martin asked Neal for his assistance to sit up. After several long minutes, Neal reluctantly complied, handing Martin the cane Sandra had brought from the plane, holding his arm until he sat up steady.

"Let's get that old banana peel off your forehead," Neal said. "Time for a new one soon, after we let your forehead breathe. Where do you think you're headed right now, Mr. Culver?"

"Gotta take a leak," Martin replied. "Which way?"

"No actual facilities," Neal replied, smirking to himself the way he often did. "You will find privacy behind that stand of sago palms to the left. Watch out for ants. On this island, guys go to the left."

"Why is that?"

"Because the women are always right," Neal replied, giggling as if he were high. "That is my feeble attempt at humor. Do you like it?"

"I have to admit, you are a funny guy," Martin said.

Martin tested his unsteady legs as he moved toward the

sago palms. By taking short steps, he covered more ground. He wore only swim trunks, the best scenario for his burns to be tended to.

Having taken care of business, Martin walked away from the camp, toward the beach.

He checked on the PBY anchoring lines. He noted that the tide was high on the beach, leaving a very narrow strip of sand. He looked down the beach as far as his eyes could see given the fading light and the mist from the crashing waves, but he did not see Sandra. The late afternoon sun would be setting soon.

What Martin did see chilled his blood, even more so when he realized that he had no idea what he was actually looking at.

As he looked to the north, a long sailboat with black sails appeared silently on the sea, passing from east to west well beyond the nose of the beached PBY plane. Martin squinted to be sure of what he was seeing. A dark fog appeared alongside the ship, which appeared to ride or coast on the fogbank.

At the bow, a single dark figure could be seen, extremely thin, clothes flapping in the breeze. The ghostly figure gazed steadily forward, seeming not to notice him at all.

Martin thought to hail the vessel, but decided against that

plan when the second chill hit him, whether due to the onset of night or the damp effect of the fog, Martin could not determine. The shadowy figure at the bow did not acknowledge him in the least.

The dark sailing sloop cruised past, contrary to the wind, moving at a phenomenal rate of speed. Its shadowy silhouette could be seen briefly before passing in front of the setting sun and disappearing.

"She'll be along soon," Neal said, causing Martin to nearly jump out of his skin. "Sandra is coming."

"I didn't hear you walk up," Martin said. "There is no one else on this island, other than the four of us?"

"No. We don't get many visitors, like I said. You two are the first in months. Did you see someone?"

"I thought I did."

"You should eat something, Mr. Culver. I'm roasting some sweet potatoes," Neal offered. "Sandra will be along any minute, I'm sure of it."

"How do you know?" Martin said. "What if something happened to her?"

Neal did not respond, finally stating, "I just know."

"What else is on this island?" Martin asked. "Any houses or labs or piers, anything?"

"The island was heavily populated at one time, not so long

ago. Life was better here than on the mainland."

"What did people here do for work? Were there job sources?"

"Let's see, they fished, grew tobacco, rolled fat cigars and had fat babies. I told you that there's an old Russian research facility on the other side of the island," Neal replied. "Weaponizing dolphins to plant mines from the 1960s to the 1980s." He shook his head in regret. "What horrible things they did."

"The good news is that the Russians left a power infrastructure, a small nuclear powerplant, capable of supplying all the buildings there with sufficient energy for lighting and their other needs."

"So you don't work over there?"

"I will go over to see Eva at times. The walk ends up being a recharge, for me. Walking keeps my joints limber. That side is where Eva does her work. "

Neal got a sheepish look on his face.

"Let me try this one out on you. Would you believe I have never been into her labs, after almost two years? Do you believe that?"

"Why?"

"She is very private. Besides, her work sounds too creepy. The Russians did brain implants, body circuits, every evil thing you could possibly subject a dolphin to."

"And now Eva subjects herself to the same treatment? Self-inflicted surgeries?" Martin inquired.

"In a nutshell, yes. It is an obsession with her. My hope is that she never finds the armory bunker. I have found it on a map and on permit notes for research on the island, mostly in Cold War archives. Every kind of bomb was used in dolphin warfare, including nuclear towables. I would not go into *that* building, if I were you."

Martin raised his eyebrows. *"Because...?"*

"Yes, Mr. Culver, if you thought they maintained fissionable material there, yes, the place is likely to be radioactive. I do not have a Gauss meter to conduct radiation tests. But even that is not the worst. The worst is "The Secret" that people who used to live here would tell in their living rooms and around their fires at night."

"What is the worst, Neal? What is this Secret?"

"Mr. Culver, before I tell you, first you must be sworn to secrecy. Secondly, I must tell you how much I enjoy engaging in conversation with you. I miss that by being here. My social skills need development. Talking to you is very important and helpful."

"Thank you, Neal. I am enjoying our conversation as well."

Neal smiled a toothy, irregular smile, pushing his glasses up on the bridge of his nose. Martin noticed that Neal did not sweat, but he did notice a slight rank odor that he could not identify. It was the hottest, most still part of the day, so he assumed there might even be something dead in the woods nearby, a wild animal perhaps.

"Rumor was," Neal continued, "that the Russians experimented on people there as well, trying to create human-robot hybrids."

"Was?" Martin asked. "You said the rumor 'was'?"

"The rumor died along with the people who lived here, therefore 'was' is the correct word. After they were gone, no one was left to keep the rumor alive."

"Where did they go Neal?"

"People die, Mr. Culver. Not everyone lives forever. This is a fact we must accept."

Martin drummed his fingers on the taut hammock cords.

"So help me understand something," Martin asked. "What then, given everything you have shared, is Eva's deal?"

"Of course, Mr. Culver. I am here to assist. Her deal, you asked? Please explain."

"Yes, what is her motivation? What is she trying to accomplish?"

"Yes, I understand now. Allow me to summarize. Firstly,

Eva seeks answers and hopes to provide solutions for the millions of humans worldwide who have suffered irreparable physical losses due to the plethora of global disasters in recent years. She does this by gleaning whatever she can find in the old dolphin research facility, sorting out between rumor and fact, between valid conclusion and absolute speculation. She is motivated to provide answers, to the point of mutilating her own body. Madame Curie, Jonas Salk and other scientists have done the same thing over time, with radiation, injections, *ad infinitum*."

"To complete my answer, for Eva, there are the junkyards. One section is old planes, the other is old boats. These are her resources, her raw materials. Materials that her grant budget will not buy."

"Before, you said. 'But no one else lives here now' ?" Martin asked as they walked back toward the camp. "Were there other humans living here when you got here?"

"Not a single human soul."

"And since you have arrived?"

"Not a single human soul has lived on this island." The smirking smile again.

"How did the boats and planes get here Neal? What about the people who lived here? Did they go to the mainland?"

"Are you ready to eat dinner, Mr. Culver? I must tend to

your meal."

"No thanks, Neal. I'm not hungry yet. I will wait for Sandra."

"Suit yourself," Neal said. "I believe that is the correct phrase when one chooses for themselves. We can finish our discussion later."

Martin stopped talking, holding up the palm of his hand to Neal. Neal started to speak until Martin gave him the look, holding up one finger to silence the talkative researcher.

"Did you hear that?" Martin asked.

"Sea birds?" Neal ventured.

"No, I heard someone calling. A woman's voice."

"Eva sings sometimes. I guess you would call it singing, although it's more like chanting or screaming, I would presume."

"There it is again," Martin said. "Please listen closely."

Neal closed his eyes tightly, as would a seven-year-old straining to listen.

"I heard it," Neal said. "That is your wife Sandra's voice."

"Help me back to the beach," Martin insisted. "Let me lean on your shoulder, I need to move quickly."

Martin leaned on Neal's shoulder, surprised at the tension of the younger man's muscles, a morbidly rigid tissue tone.

Returning to the water's edge, Martin and Neal watched as

far as they could see in the direction Sandra had taken. Soon Martin saw a tiny flashing, swaying light.

"Sandra, over here!" Martin shouted. "We're over here!"

"Martin!" came the lowest volume plea for help Martin had ever heard. "Help me, Martin!" Now Sandra could be heard over the sound of waves breaking along the shore.

"I'm here!" Martin shouted. "You've made it back. I'm here!"

Martin took a few halting steps toward the voice in the dark, no longer leaning on Neal. The swinging light grew brighter. Out of the darkness, Martin could see the underbrim of Sandra's large sunhat, her upper body defined by the light hanging around her neck. Her face was uplit, the shadows of her face shifting as the light around her neck swung to and fro.

Sandra looked exhausted. She was dirty and wet from head to toe, her legs were scraped and bruised. Martin noticed that she had on the ripped shirt but did not comment. She bled from any number of scratches and cuts. Her legs were black with smashed mosquitos. She could barely walk, even using her walking stick. Martin reached Sandra and they gently hugged. She was soaking wet, shivering in the night air.

"I was really worried about you," Martin said. "You must

have had a really bad time. Are you ok?"

"Yes, I'll be all right," Sandra said, refusing to cry. "I'm so tired. I almost got trapped in a cave, then I walked in the water to keep the mosquitoes away, but the tide came in, then the sun went down, and I was afraid I would never find you. My legs feel so weak."

"Let's get back to camp," Martin said. "You need the hammock more than I do right now."

Sandra limped beside Martin, then stopped. Neal returned to camp ahead of them, marching mechanically onward.

"Martin, I found something awesome," Sandra said. "I found a cave with gold coins and an oilskin packet that I think is a book and I found a galleon and…"

"Hold on, hold on," Martin responded. "You are going too fast. Let's sit down, Neal has baked some sweet potatoes. Let's eat first, then there will be time for stories."

"You are right. Martin, I was so scared."

"No need to be scared now," Martin said to reassure them both, after everything he had been hearing from Neal.

"Ok, let's eat," Sandra said. "But I need to change clothes first. Priority one is to get out of this damp bathing suit, then I need to put something on these bug bites. And I'm changing in the PBY, not in the peep show hut."

An hour later, the atmosphere in the camp was much more

relaxed. Sandra had changed clothes, slathered her legs in Neal's aloe blend, finished two sweet potatoes, some baked fish and three glasses of water. She was now stretched out in the hammock Martin had occupied earlier in the day.

"Start from the beginning," Martin said. "I want to hear everything."

"Where is Neal?" she asked, eyes darting to and fro.

"I don't know," Martin said. "He may have walked over to Eva's. Gone since dinner, though."

"Martin, I hiked around to the other side of the island. Took me about an hour," Sandra said. "I found some caves. At the mouth of the main cave I found two gold coins in a stream. One was a 1717 gold doubloon, a two escudo. They were beautiful."

"Let's see them," Martin said, moving towards the edge of his seat.

"I lost them, but I'll go back for them," she said. "I'm betting there are more."

"You lost two gold coins?"

"So you never lost anything? They fell out of my bikini top when I took it off."

"This sounds like a good story," Martin said. "Or should I wait for the movie?"

"Martin when I realized I had dropped them there was a

scorpion at the top of my walking stick at least a foot long. It was huge!" She demonstrated by holding her hands apart.

"And you were topless," Martin laughed. "How exciting!"

Sandra pouted but did not reply.

"So, new topic. Tell me about this little oil-cloth bundle you brought back," Martin said. "Can we open it?"

"Yes, let's open it," Sandra agreed. "It's in my backpack. But what if Neal comes back?"

"Yeah, about that. Where are we going to sleep tonight?"

"We could sleep here, but there's not enough beds."

"I want to sleep on the PBY," Sandra said. "The queen inflator bed is already made up and ready."

"Then let's go. Bring your backpack, I've got the light."

Chapter 10

The Pyrate Scrybe

The next morning, Martin and Sandy sat at the outdoor picnic table under a small, thatched roof, their treasures spread before them like pirates divvying up a pile of booty.

"Costa Rican breakfast, coffee and bananas, not bad," Martin commented. "Tastes even better with you here."

"I need more coffee," Sandra smiled, getting up. Suddenly Neal was standing next to her, coffee pot in hand, silent. Sandra sat back down as Neal neatly filled her cup.

"Are we ready to open it?" Martin asked, placing the oil cloth bundle on the small table.

He could see Neal watching from the kitchen area.

"Yes, I think we've waited long enough."

"I don't think you should open that," Neal said bluntly. "I think it was there all this time for a reason. Humans should not disturb things they find. Maybe it's cursed. Everything else in the *Cueva de Eva* is cursed. Maybe we will all be cursed if you open it."

"Neal, I did not take you for a superstitious man," Sandra replied. "I see you as more factual, more scientific. But we are going to find out what this is, if we can."

"Then I'm out. I'm leaving. I want no part of that, whoever is listening, I'm not a part of this." Neal left, walking along the inclined path to the center of the island. His fingers were in his ears.

"So, acceptable behavior here is that if we get tense, we just walk out? New strategy. I must remember it," Martin said. " 'Whoever is listening?' What was that about?"

"Martin, try not to be so harsh," Sandra chided. "He's different."

"You said a mouthful there. Here, put these on," Martin instructed. He gloved up, then handed Sandra two surgical gloves from Neal's research kit. "We handle this artifact with the utmost care, ok?"

Sandra took a dull kitchen knife from the food table bin and began sawing at the leather binding.

"No wait!" Martin interjected. "There's a better way. I already checked."

Bringing out a small tin of machine oil, Martin placed a drop at a time on the knot holding the leather binding in place.

Using two pointed sticks also lubricated with the oil, Martin gently probed the knot, working it loose one strand of leather sinew at a time. Sandra moved to a position where

Martin could have more light.

"Now," Martin said, "you take over. I'm not great with the fine motor skills yet. This is your prize. You found it and recovered it. You should be the first to see it. That way, if it's a bundle of scorpions, I will be safer over here."

Sandra smiled a wry smile as they switched seats. She followed Martin's lead, oiling and lifting each centimeter of the leather binding before peeling it back. She blew back a strand of hair from her face, biting her lower lip as she concentrated on the task. Little by little, the binding released its hold, leaving a dark tannin stain where it had been wound around the oilskin.

"So what is oilskin?" Sandra asked. " It kind of stinks."

"Oilskin is cloth treated with oil to make it waterproof. The first raingear used by sailing captains after actual skins was oilcloth. The smell is from the oil. Probably whale oil."

The oilskin peeled away from what it protected like a leathery onion one layer at a time. Eventually, what lay before them was a stack of ancient written documents, rendered in the most elegant hand. They were written in English.

"See, no scorpions," Sandra said.

"Looks like letters or pamphlets," Martin said.

"Pamphlets?"

"An early name for books. Short books or treatises on certain topics. They look a little thick for individual letters."

"This top one is sealed with a blob of black wax," Sandra said. "The wax seal reads P.S. in the center. There is another more cryptic seal stamped into the leather. Odd lettering I don't recognize. But the wax seal has separated from one side of the paper, so it won't hurt to open it, right?"

"I wonder what curious details these documents contain," she said as she carefully unfolded the ancient paper.

Martin watched intently. He was dying to help, but he waited as Sandra methodically worked.

"This top one is a collection, a group of smaller written documents topping off the bundle. They are in really good shape, and apparently more recent."

"Let's keep them in order in case they are not dated."

"The paper feels like cloth."

"Paper in the 1700 and 1800's was heavy in rag or cotton content. Made from old clothes, sheets and so on, seldom new cotton. Beaten for days to reduce it down to a fine pulp."

"I remember seeing something about the rag content of paper when I was younger."

"Exactly," Martin said. "Paper from trees was a recent Western development. Good for us, since the older rag paper survives longer."

"The one letter on the top is the most recent. It's dated 1827."

"Go ahead, read it if you can."

Sandra squinted at the paper. "Weird lettering they used, all of the "S" letters are written like "F's."

"Do you need more time?"

"No, I'm ready. Here goes."

"To whom it may concern,
By removing thif bundle from itf refting place.
bye opening it, you have traded your peace for problemf.
I do not place a curfe upon you,
rather I tell you in all honestye
that the talef contained in these letterf
will disturb your dreams,
leave you hoping for the dawn.
In thif place of nyghtmaref, as in no other,
dreams never, never come true,
as faythfullye recorded in these talef.
Figned, the Pyrate Fcribe."

"Such a challenge to read," Martin stated. He leaned back in his chair, noting that for once the chair back did not hurt his scorched shoulder. "*Never, never* come true, like in

Neverland?"

"Stop joking Martin. It's a warning, a curse. I should not have opened it. I should have left it there. Neal warned us. I don't know what made me take it."

"Relax, Sandra. It's 18th Century propaganda," Martin laughed. "It sounds like a great promo to pitch to a publisher, amping up the drama to sell a story."

"Martin, seriously. Trouble follows you wherever you go, and now we are cursed because of something foolish I did. Is it never going to end?"

Martin laughed softly. "The only foolish thing you did was to go roaming around in that cave topless, with a million scorpions ogling you with their beady little eyes."

Sandra shivered. "Please don't remind me."

"So the next page is pretty hard to read, but it looks like it says "Code of the Pyrate Brethren". That is lettered large. Must be like the title. Below that it reads in smaller lettering:

"Collected Talef of Adventurerf and Bouccaneerf
of the Caribbean at Great Hardfhip
of Life, Limb, and Liberty.
Signed, The Pyrate Fcribe."

Martin leaned further back in his chair. "Maybe you're

right, maybe we shouldn't open this. I have a bad feeling about it."

"Are you serious?" Sandra said, wide-eyed.

"Of course not, are you kidding? Pass them over here, I'm ready to dig into this little mystery."

As Sandra gathered the next bundle to hand to Martin, she grimaced first, then screamed.

"Ow, ow, ow," she shouted, dropping the pages to the table.

Sandra flicked her wrist rapidly, as if trying to shake something off of her hand.

"Ow, a scorpion, Martin! Kill it!"

Martin instinctively looked to the ground, raising his walking stick as soon as he located the insect. Pinning the offending arachnid with the second stab, Martin ground the insect into the dirt. An acrid smell permeated the area beneath the table.

"Where did it bite you?" Martin asked.

"Sting is the proper term," Neal said. "You killed it? Scorpions to not have the ability to bite humans. They have no actual teeth, however their tail..."

"Neal, I'm glad you came back, but hold the facts, ok? Let's help Sandra, will you? Do you have that pain medicine handy?"

"I have a sufficient quantity to assist Sandra...Mrs. Culver, and yes, I will assist her. Sandra, please lie back in this hammock and raise your hand over your head."

Sandra did as he asked, slipping into the hammock as she gripped her injured wrist.

"There, there your blouse has come undone," Neal said, "Allow me to..."

"Neal, forget that! The pain medicine! Please don't make me wait."

Neal reached to grip Sandra's wrist with one hand, while administering the pain injection into the muscle of her forearm. His grip was a tight as his face was tense, until the pain injection was complete.

Sandra's face visibly relaxed within seconds. Her forearm and hand grew less tense. Within less than a minute she was breathing easier, her shoulders going limp as she melted into the hammock.

"Just relax," Neal advised, his voice calm and quiet.

Sandra's eyelids blinked twice before she leaned her head against the taught woven hammock and went to sleep.

"There, that's better," Neal stated. "Mr. Culver, Sandra will sleep for a few hours, perhaps as little as one to two hours. Will you come close her blouse? Two buttons appear to have come undone. I can see..."

"You've done enough for now, Neal."

"Did you give her too much?" Martin asked. "She is out!"

"I administered the same amount that I did for you Mr. Martin Culver. Is that not correct?"

"You have a lot to learn about working with humans, Neal!" Martin said in his most commanding voice. "She only weighs half as much as I do. You must adjust for body weight."

"There is no need for anger, Mr. Martin Culver. She will sleep through it, perhaps for a little longer."

Martin squeezed past Neal, noting the researchers defensive and inappropriate gaze toward Sandra. Martin closed Sandra's blouse buttons, turned, and found that Neal had disappeared again.

Chapter 11

The Code of the Brethren

"So who wrote the Pirate Code of the Brethren anyway, this Pyrate Scrybe? Whoever he is?"

"I did not know you were awake," Martin said. "Only an hour has passed. How do you feel?"

"Drunk," she replied, flexing her fingers as she sat up in the hammock. "Tipsy. My wrist doesn't hurt though. Just a small red mark where it bit me."

"Stung," Martin corrected. "I killed it for stinging you."

"Whatever... bit, stung, all I know is that it hurt. It hurt a lot."

"We can wait till later to go over these papers. I've been doing some reading while you were taking a nap."

"I was recovering, thank you very much. And yes, I still want to know if the Pyrate Scrybe wrote the Code of the Brethren."

"No, he likely just recorded it, but he may have been present at one of the great pirate councils where it was discussed. The largest council ever was held in Port Royal."

"Could be a she, I'm just sayin'," Sandra commented. "So

what does it say?"

"It's interesting. Surprisingly simple, fair statements. Pirates Morgan and Bartholomew led the pirate court in hashing out these rules. The Pyrate Scrybe, whoever he is, recorded the statements. Pirates lived by these as a code of conduct, laws more or less."

"The Pyrate Scrybe may have even been a Keeper of the Code. The Code was considered important enough that copies of it were entrusted to certain individuals for safekeeping. Literacy was scarce, and was an important qualification for the Code Keepers."

"Once adopted by the Council, pirate Captains would shoot anyone who dared speak poorly of the Code or its tenets. The Keeper of the Code had the right to insist that the Code serve as law. The Code allowed that the real code is in a pirate's heart, the true guide for a man of the sea as to what he can do and what he can't do."

"So, what are the rules?" Sandra asked. "Give me an example."

"Here goes," Martin said. " 'Rule one, Befriend others wisely'."

"Sounds like this means be cautious in adding friends," Sandra commented.

"Two," Martin continued. "The right of Parlay. The term

"Parlay" or "Parley" was written in the Pirata Codex. Parlay was known as a right in the Code of the Pirate Brethren, as set down by Morgan and Bartholomew. It allowed any detained person to invoke temporary protection before the ship captain to negotiate without being attacked until the parlay was complete. Parlay is invoked simply by saying the word aloud. Many a Code hearing was frustrated and confused by this word. It almost defies logic to use it. As if you can stop a sword or a plank walk with a word."

"Makes sure your argument gets heard, I like it. Go on," Sandra said. "This is getting interesting."

"Three. When a pirate is to be marooned, for an offense which does not deserve death, they are to be given bread or hardtack, a bottle of water (if any exist), and a pistol loaded with a single shot."

"It gets kind of technical after that," Martin said. "For example, Article II, Section I, Paragraph VIII, sharing of the spoils, and Article II, Section II, Paragraph I whoever first spotted a treasure-laden ship could choose the best pistol for themselves. The best of anything on the ship for that matter."

"Oh, what does it say about dividing up treasure?" Sandra asked. "If we go back to that cave, I need to how to split what we're going to bring out."

"Here is the rest in a nutshell," Martin said. "Every crew

member is to have an equal share in any treasure found."

"What else?"

"Any man who falls behind is left behind."

"Uh-oh, does that give you the right to leave me behind, now that I am injured?"

Martin continued without comment, noting Sandra's closed eyes.

"Knowingly targeting and sinking other pirate ships is strictly forbidden."

Sandra initially made no response. "Who sank the ship I saw in the cave?"

"Next there is a list of real life or death matters," Martin read. "These guys were tough. Betrayal is punishable by death. Any person who refuses to serve aboard a pirate ship may be killed. Killing a surrendered enemy is not allowed."

"Sounds like a very complete list," Sandra said, yawning.

"The Code also contained strict regulations on eyepatch color."

"Oh no, not a pirate's style guide. Now I have heard it all."

"You are talking gibberish," Neal said, without notice. "They were obviously trying to establish some uniformity and structure over a very diverse group of wild and unstructured men. I can see many uses for this."

"Sounds like some people I knew growing up," Sandra

said. "Wild and unstructured men, ha!"

"One last one, "Martin said. "A pirate never gives another over to the authorities. Then it reads, 'See Betrayal'."

"Yep, just like those people in high school, always ratting us out for the things we did. Oops, did I say that out loud?"

Martin stopped to contemplate whether the pain compound Neal had produced had any effect as a truth serum.

"What type of things were they ratting you out about?" Martin asked, probing his theory.

"Interesting stuff," Sandra said haughtily. "Stuff I probably never told *you* about. A good girl can have a fun past, you know."

"Go on," Martin said.

"No," Sandra said. "Anything in there about walking the plank?"

"No, I didn't see it, though it's probably in here somewhere."

"I never walked a plank," Sandra laughed. "So I wasn't *that bad*."

"I do think you are drunk, though," Martin agreed.

"I've been drunk before," Sandra laughed. "Might happen again."

"Sandra, I don't know if you realize what a treasure this

bundle is? A hand-lettered first-person account of the Code of the Pirate Brethren. These documents are no doubt priceless to the right collector."

"What else is in there? The rest of the packet, not the rules."

"It appears to be a series of individual pirate histories," Martin said. "One history for each of the Nine Pirate Lords. The first contains the account of one Jose Gaspar, the Gentleman Pyrate from Spain, who ruled the waters from Tampa to Havana for years. His base was on this very island, Scorpion Key, as it was noted on the early maps. Gaspar was a very prolific pirate, both in terms of taking gold and of leaving heirs. He was also a very private man, keeping a low profile, leaving little in the historical record. What we do know about him comes from third-hand accounts, 'I-knew-a-guy-who-said-so', that kind of thing. Captain Pierre Lafitte contributed a lot of the details."

"What happened to Gaspar?"

"The story reads as if Gaspar faked his death to get away from his many wives and children. Supposedly he was cornered by an American warship near the Marquesas, where he tied himself to an anchor and sank to the bottom rather than be captured. This says his body was never found, officially."

"Other accounts say Lafitte rescued Gaspar, then killed him, buried his body and stole his treasure. He apparently wooed Taina, the woman that the two Captains shared."

The account says that Taina found out about Gaspar and the treasure, dooming Lafitte to spend eternity with Gaspar's bones. Lafitte, known as the most vain of all pirates, was permitted to keep his many rings in exile, one for each finger, and two for each thumb."

Martin looked to find Sandra sleeping again. He read on silently through the afternoon.

Chapter 12

An Unexpected Visitor

At the exact moment that sunset normally occurred, Jack Culver found himself peering through sheets of pouring rain, watching a thin, cloaked figure step off the longest sailboat Jack had ever seen, onto his newly completed concrete boat dock made from concrete manually mixed and poured to an exact and impressive 35 meters.

Having cooked dinner for Enrique and Elizabeth, Jack had just stepped out on the veranda for a smoke. He put out his cigarette midway through, upon seeing this person set foot on his dock not one hundred feet below, down four levels of stairs to the rocky Pacific coastline.

Moving unsteadily through the tropical downpour, the figure leaned heavily on a stout silver cane that reflected the lights from every window in Jack's seaside villa. While Jack felt that he understood somewhat, that feeling of waiting for your "land-legs" to return after an extended time at sea, something about this visitor raised the hair on his neck.

Yet Jack knew nothing of this arrival at the new pier of his Pacific resort in Costa Rica, other than it was the first boat to arrive since the completion of the construction project. With things the way they were in the world, Jack had no real way of "advertising" to let anyone know of the availability of this new boat dock, or of his former five-star resort. For this arrival, Jack had received no warning, no advance word, no prior contact. Now the ominous craft was here without a single marking or flag to indicate provenance of this mysterious boat.

The imposing vessel seemed to hover motionless alongside the dock, riding light on the rough surface as might a tethered helium balloon on a gentle breeze. Measuring the length of the concrete pier where it now was docked, no lights appeared anywhere on this boat.

Jack stood from his chair on the covered porch, peering between showers for a better look. For a moment, Jack wondered how the vessel had sailed into the cove and docked without lights. Like some black waterborne hearse, the mere sight of this boat gave Jack the chills. Though waves from the storm pounded the dock, the sailboat barely moved.

Eyeing the figure making its way along the newly constructed pier, Jack considered who might have so expertly tied the craft off. The sails of the tremendous sloop, which had also been properly secured, were as dark as this ghostly person's cloak, darker than the coming night.

Before long, it became obvious that the dark, dripping cloak clung to a *woman's* body, though not in a way one would consider attractive. Her walk seemed stilted, not quite a limp, as if her joints were unable to bend. The material encasing the woman's legs revealed them to be thin and not the least bit shapely. The only thing that distinguished the figure as female were muscular breasts and hips readily visible through the soaked cloth of her cloak. Though feminine, both areas appeared more those of an athlete than a fashion model.

"Halt, who goes there?" Jack snarled into the night. Reaching the end of the dock nearest land, the figure stopped walking.

Receiving no response, Jack leveled his shotgun to his shoulder and fired over the intruder's head. Shotgun pellets rained down around the person standing just out of the weapon's range.

"Move again and I'll fill you full of holes," Jack called out.

Jack moved the warm shotgun barrel to the crook of his left arm, shining a spotlight down the slight hill toward the dock.

The figure took two steps forward, then looked up into the glare of Jack's floodlight. Only her heavily scarred chin was visible as the rain poured over the ragged hood of her cloak.

"I came to see Elizabeth," the ghostly figure croaked.

"Go back to hell," Jack shouted. "You're not seeing anyone!"

"I'm here with a warning," the voice replied.

"You and what three ghosts?" Jack Culver barked back.

"I came a long way to warn you," the intruder continued. "I've fought hell and blazes to be here. Make jokes if you must, but you will be the one to suffer."

The voice was horrible: broken, forlorn and haunting. "I have come to warn you. Heed my words or find your days numbered! Then I will come for you, and you will go with me."

Jack shivered, the chill of the rain, he told himself, feeling that he should recognize the voice, but he could not place it. He grew tired of the banter, remaining unafraid of the threat.

"Get the hell off my pier," Jack called. With that, he fired the shotgun again, aiming lower than before. The figure turned away, stumbled, then fell to their knees.

"I've got responsibilities here. I'm not going anywhere with you, now or anytime, and neither is anyone else!"

As Jack watched, the figure leaned heavily on their cane with both arms, standing to their feet before inching down the dock toward the boat. Jack saw a trail of dark blood stain the water puddles on the new dock before being diluted and dissipated by the sudden, swift rain.

"At least whatever it is was physical, not mental," Jack reassured himself. "I thought I was going crazy for a minute," he said out loud.

"Your time is limited, Jack Culver," the voice called back. The figure flowed up onto the boat and across the bow. Slowly the vessel pulled away, disappearing into the dark rain.

"Who was that, Grandpa Jack?" Enrique asked from the doorway. "I heard the shotgun go off. Two times."

"I did not see you standing there," Jack said. "I'm sorry you had to hear that. What did you see?"

"I saw a shadow, on a shadow boat," Enrique said. "I wasn't scared, because you were here. You made them leave."

"Good boy," Jack said. "That's all it was. A shadow. Let's go inside, it's chilly out here."

Chapter 13

Gaspar's Galleon

Martin paused, realizing he was once again walking far ahead of Sandra.

"I can't keep up with you today," Sandra said, smiling as she bounced cheerily up the beach to plant a very light kiss on Martin's healing cheek. "You're definitely getting your energy back. Of course, I've known that since the sun came up today."

Martin smiled a smile that Sandra recognized. She blushed.

"That *was* nice," Martin agreed. "Time with you *renews* my energy. Then again, I'm also really excited to see this cave you have said so much about. I know it seems like I am rushing, but by the time we reach the entrance, we will only have about an hour before the tide comes back in, so I want to get there as soon as we can."

"We're not far now," Sandra said. "From here you can see the bushes that I told you about, that form a "V" over the cave entrance? Between the two sand mounds that look like thighs. Do you see what I'm talking about?"

Martin looked in the direction Sandra pointed. True to her description, the entrance to the *Cueva de Eva* appeared to be a voluptuous woman lying on her back.

"How could I not see it?" Martin said. "The resemblance is striking. The "V" formed by the undergrowth resembled a triangle pointing down. Martin could definitely see the resemblance to female anatomy that Sandra had described.

"So in this case, "V" marks the spot, not "X" ?" Martin quipped. He waited for her response.

"Enough with the jokes, mister. Go back to walking faster, now that you can see where we're headed." Martin took her instructions literally, rushing ahead, nearly running, despite wearing his heavy boots.

Minutes later, as Sandra caught up, she found Martin on his knees at the mouth of the cave, digging furiously. The outgoing tide was draining water from the cave, creating an outflow stream that carried away most of the sand burden, exposing numerous gold coins.

"Look what I found," Martin exclaimed. "I probed with my hiking stick where you said. I think I hit the jackpot." He held up a net bag weighed down with gold doubloons. "There's a half pound of gold here. I found 16 coins!"

Sandra helped Martin to his feet. "Told you." she said simply.

The climate changed the moment they stepped inside the cave. The temperature dropped 20 degrees. From an early morning sauna to an evening-like chill, the difference was literally night and day.

"The sand is hard packed underneath," Martin commented, noting that they were barely leaving footprints, which filled with water but immediately drained. "This water is fresh, with a good rate of flow."

"This is the ideal time to come here, apparently," Sandra mused. "While the tide is low. An hour from now we do not want to be here. The tide will come in and scorpions will crawl out of every crack in these rocks."

Martin twisted the dial on his watch, timing their exit for exactly 55 minutes.

"Do you see any scorpions?" Martin asked. "I brought a black light to spot them, just in case."

"Not yet," Sandra said. "Here is the spot I drew on the map. I call it *Playita*, the mini-beach. This is where I lost the two coins."

Sunlight streamed into the cave from the circular opening at the top of the cave, illuminating the two coins on the sand, lying where she had dropped them. This time Sandra popped the coins into a zippered pouch around her neck.

"The sun will only last here for a moment," Sandra said.

"It is like a special place in space and time."

"So this is where you stripped down?" Martin asked.

Sandra stared at him over her sunglasses before removing them.

"A bit chilly, was it?" he joked.

"Change the subject, will you? I was up to my chest in freezing water. I was wet and chilly, with water so cold I felt warmer without a damp bathing suit. I brought a t-shirt like you said.

"Okay, okay," Martin replied. "Where is this shelf you were talking about?"

"Up here," Sandra said, moving up the slight incline to the back of the cave. "Be careful, it's still wet, so it's slippery. The algae is still draining water."

Martin moved to where Sandra stood. At first the area appeared to be a blank wall, with only the slightest hint of a shelf or indentation. As Martin's eyes adjusted, he became fascinated with what they were seeing.

"First of all, these are tool marks along the edges, so this is not a natural alcove. It is very interesting how it does not look indented from the front, yet along the sides it can be seen to be half a meter deep. That would make it look like the bundle was floating in thin air, to anyone who rowed or waded in here. At high tide no one could even make it inside.

What else sat on this shelf?"

"When I was here, nothing but rats," Sandra remarked, shivering. "I screamed. They did too!"

Martin traced his flashlight along the shelf, examining the trash piles left by the rats. He stepped back. The wall revealed faded paint outlining a man's face with dark eyes and hair, definite Spanish features.

"You didn't mention this portrait," Martin said. "Who is this?"

"Looks Spanish, so I would say Gaspar," Sandra said.

"Why paint his picture here?" Martin asked. "No one's going to see it."

"We're seeing it," Sandra reminded him. "To guard his tomb? Is that what this is?"

"Good question," Martin agreed. He continued to poke through the debris left by the rats. "Or to mark a grave. *Las Tumbas* caves, remember? That means "The Tombs" in Spanish."

Martin grew quiet as he pored over the items on the shelf.

"We are so lucky," Martin said in a low voice. "These are true packrats."

"Don't I know it," Sandra said. "Try not to breathe the dust, though."

Martin used the point of his knife to probe the packrat

piles.

"Packrats are important to archaeologists because they gather things, and they can get into tiny areas that other animals cannot. Plus they like shiny stuff, so the treasure potential of any site can be instantly evaluated by what is found in a packrat nest."

"Well, what do you find there, Mr. Packrat-Expert? Don't forget to keep an eye on our time. I will watch the cave entrance."

"Perfect," Martin said. "So here is what I see. I think you will be happy. Two large pearls, one white and one grey, a small gold cross in 17th century Spanish style, a couple of pieces of deep green sea-glass, and finally, three gold coins. And this old key."

"Grey pearls are from the Pacific," Sandra said. "My parents bought some from a vendor in Peru. Wonder what lock that key might fit?"

"More importantly, there is a close-by source of these items," Martin said gleefully. "They had to come from somewhere nearby. There should be more around here somewhere. These are not likely to be flotsam or jetsam."

"Huh?"

"These items did not just wash in on the tide," Martin said. "Except for possibly the pieces of sea glass. We are on the track of a treasure with gold coins, pearls and Spanish objects."

"So if these items didn't wash in, where did they come from?" Sandra asked. "Oh, I forgot to check. The tide has stopped going out."

"We have 40 minutes," Martin said. "Let's look around. Did you say the letter about Gaspar mentioned another cave behind this one?"

"Yes. It says that when you look at wall, there is an area that resembles a woman's rump."

"Not just any rump?" Martin asked, teasing.

"It specifically said the wall over the entrance resembled a woman's rump. But you know old sailors. They thought manatees were mermaids. They might try to date an oak barrel for all I know. So their concept of a woman's rump may be subjective."

Martin stepped back from the shelf.

"All we have found that is man-made is this shelf, which sits above the high-tide line," Martin said. "So if I were to start anywhere…"

Sandra stepped back. "Martin. Martin."

"What is it?" Martin asked. "What do you see?"

"Beside your foot. A huge scorpion. Don't move."

Martin looked down to see the largest scorpion he had

ever laid eyes on. He did not recall seeing one this large in any nature documentary. The front pincers were open, while the tail reared above the thorax like a venomous whip. The pincers and tail rose almost to his knee.

"What are you going to do?"

"I don't have much choice, unless you brought the *escopeta*," Martin replied nervously.

"A shotgun? I don't have…oh yeah, we do, on the plane. Should I go get it?"

"No," Martin said. "Don't move. But when I tell you to, I want you to wave your arms and make some noise. I will take care of the rest. Ready. I'll say NOW!"

"Okay, I'm ready. You say when."

Martin reached slowly forward to the point where he had leaned his hiking stick against the cavern wall. "I'm going to try to bat this scary P.O.S. into the next life," Martin said. "I can only do it one-handed and I only have one chance. Ready?"

"Ready. Good luck." Sandra turned her head away.

"NOW!" Martin shouted. His grip on the hiking stick was firm as Sandra waved her arms and shouted. Swinging the stick a full 180 degrees with his right hand, he connected with the confused arachnid mid-thorax, but the scorpion did not go sailing as planned. It simply latched onto the stick, wagging its tail as if taunting Martin. Then it started scurrying up the stick towards Martin's hand. Martin heard Sandra scream.

Swinging the stick in a circle, Martin used centrifugal force to keep the scorpion at arms-length from his body. The scorpion scrambled to hold on, clicking as it moved. It held on just long enough for Martin to release the hiking stick into the darkest corner of the cavern, where it clattered with the sound of wood rattling on wood.

Martin's epic toss was at least 100 feet. Martin later swore that he heard that scorpion hiss like a snake as it reached escape velocity, but that was not the strangest sound that was heard echoing through the cave.

The clatter of wood on wood had been unmistakable. Martin's hiking stick had collided with something wooden in the darker reaches of the rocky cave. Yet it was too dark and too deep to be seen.

"Did you hear that?" Martin asked. "What was it?"

"My wandering ghost ship that moves in and out on the tide, perhaps?" Sandra offered.

"Very funny," Martin said. "If said ghost ship exists, we have to make a choice. We have 25 minutes left until we sprint for the daylight," he said.

"Gaspar's Galleon," Sandra laughed. "It's there all right."

"I'd rather try to figure out this second cave thing," she said.

"Okay, I can look for my hiking stick another day. I really don't want to go over there in the dark with that scorpion anyway."

"Martin. Martin."

"Not again," he said.

"No, look up. Stop where you are and look up, about ten feet above the shelf indentation. From where I am standing, I see what we are looking for."

Martin looked up, and for the world, it looked as if he were seeing a sculptured feminine rear, on a wall formed by purely geological forces.

"That's her," Martin shouted. "But where's the second cave?"

"You said, 'that's her'," Sandra laughed. "You mean that's it, am I right?"

"Yes,... her,... it,... I am feeling a little pressure here, before we run out of time. Let me look at the shelf again."

Martin approached the wall, checking his watch. "Twenty minutes," he said to no one in particular. He began to examine the wall and the floor of the cave more closely.

What he had originally taken to be packrat midden droppings were possibly a type of plaster, Martin concluded. He pulled out his knife, tracing a pattern around the two meter wide, three meter high shelf.

"Sandra, come over here and hold the light," Martin asked. "I think I may have found something." Martin handed Sandra his flashlight, probing deeper with his knife.

"I know this is not good archaeology," he apologized. "There is no one to report it to anyway. But I think there is something behind this wall. That is why the warning letter was inserted into the oilcloth letter bundle, to scare people away. Away from what, I don't know."

Abruptly Martin's probing knife sank completely into the wall, disappearing to the very hilt. Fine white dust poured loosely onto the shelf, creating a choking cloud that blocked all available light, including the couple's view of each other. Sandra immediately went into coughing fits. Martin held his breath as long as he could, but his eyes burned, tears welling up uncontrollably in his eyes.

As the dust began to settle, it coated everything in a thin layer of white as far as their eyes could see. Sandra's laughter echoed through the cave between coughing spasms..

"You look like a ghost," Sandra giggled, still coughing. "The plaster is all over you."

"I actually think it's flour," Martin said. "Some got in my mouth. It's not salty like plaster. But that was quite a surprise. I wonder if it was a booby trap?"

"Obviously," Sandra said. "And being enclosed in the wall kept it dry for all this time."

Martin looked at his watch. They had 10 minutes left, and were mere minutes from a major new discovery, but sea water was starting to enter the cave.

"Speaking of how long, it's almost time to leave. Let's collect our things. No one else is coming in here before we come back. We only have one way out."

We always have the opening in the ceiling of the cave," Sandra reminded. "But unless you have climbing gear in that backpack, which I doubt…"

"Correct as usual, but let's not go there. It is too high for us to jump. The water will never rise high enough for us to escape that way. Better to go out the same door we entered."

Sandra looked up to the woman's rump landmark. "I want to name our landmark, but I can't think of anything appropriate."

"*Trasera de Eva,*" Martin said. "If we are in the *Cueva de Eva*, that must be the *trasera*, the portion *atras*. Don't you agree?"

"Okay, agreed," Sandra finally said, rolling her eyes in the dim light as she led the way. "Let's just get out of here. I'm feeling panicky. We're almost too late."

Sandra and Martin moved carefully down the slippery

rocks toward the mouth of the cave, then Sandra stopped in her tracks.

"What is it?" Martin asked, trying to see around Sandra. The last rays of sunlight were streaking across the cave, nearly blinding him.

"Scorpions," Sandra said. "A lot of them."

"Quit kidding," Martin said. "I'm ready to go. I want to wash off this flour dust or whatever it is."

"I can't go any further, Martin. Really. Just below us is the place where I slipped and fell. The slope gets even steeper. There are too many of them for us to try to go around."

Martin pulled out his blacklight flashlight. He leaned over Sandra's shoulder with the UV light.

"Damn," he agreed. "That's a lot of scorpions."

The floor of the cave between the rising waves and where they stood literally crawled with scorpions of all sizes. Some scorpions were covered with dozens of smaller scorpions, babies carried by their mothers. Others were huge. All had pincers raised with their tails in attack position. And all showed bluish-green under UV light.

"Okay, so we move back," Martin said. "Back to the shelf alcove for now."

"We can't go further into the cave," Sandra said. "We need to get out. Martin I'm scared."

"It's going to be okay," Martin replied, doing his best to reassure them both. "If we have to, we can sit up on the niche shelf and wait the tide out. There is room enough to sit or stand up there."

"As long as the rats don't come back," Sandra worried. "I'll scream so loud."

"We're going to be okay," Martin repeated. He did not believe himself any more the second time he said it than the first.

Reaching the back wall of the cave, Martin cleared the shelf, pushing everything to one side. He laced his fingers to make a foothold for Sandra to step up and take a seat on the rough shelf.

"They're coming, Martin. Get up here."

Martin swung his backpack off, swinging it up onto the shelf. They were both surprised to hear a hollow thump, as if Martin had banged on an old wooden door.

"Now, what was that?" Martin asked.

"Get up here first," Sandra pleaded. "Then you can check it out."

Martin placed his hands on the shelf, pushing himself up and onto its relative safety. Again, the seeming rock wall thumped with a hollow sound. Scorpions swarmed all around where Martin's feet had stood, as if trying to absorb his warmth.

"What is up with this wall?" Martin asked. "Sounds like wood, not rock."

"Do you really feel that is our biggest problem right now?" Sandra asked. "It seems to me that our being stuck in this cave with the tide coming in and hungry scorpions eyeing us for dinner might be bigger concerns?"

"You are right, of course," Martin replied. "But we might be able to deal with both concerns if my guess is right. First off, the scorpions are not climbing his wall, since it is smooth plaster. See how they are falling back down? That's probably why the rats nested up here. The oilcloth letters survived up here, too."

Martin inserted his knife into the same hole that he had made earlier. He began to work up and down until he had dislodged all the flour plaster along one side of the shelf indentation.

"Noisy for a second," he warned Sandra, who amused herself by pushing piles of flour dust onto the hundreds of scorpions milling about, only four feet below them. The scorpions did their best to avoid the powder, but were noticeably more active, the darker it got in the cave. She pulled her feet up onto the shelf.

Martin slammed his elbow as hard as he could against the

back wall of the shallow grotto. When he did, a crack opened up around the entire inner border of the shelf indentation, giving him a degree of hope. Since Martin had run his knife down the entire right side of the niche, he guessed that to be the side to open, if any would, since there were no hinges anywhere along its length.

Martin quickly scoured away the plaster at the edge of the shelf along the top and the bottom, working around Sandra's backside while she perched on her feet like a bird in a cage.

"Martin, the scorpions have figured out how to stack up on top of each other. They are coming closer. Can you work faster, please? I have to pee. All this excitement."

"Working as fast as I can here. More noise," Martin warned. He slammed the wall with his elbow again, the echo overpowering the sound of rising water and hissing scorpions. The wall moved nearly half an inch on three sides.

"Sandra, I have an idea. Why not pee on those scorpions? Human urine repels a lot of pests. Unless you've got a lighter and some matches inside that bathing suit, which I doubt..."

"Yeah, right," Sandra giggled. "You are still thinking how to get me undressed in this cave aren't you? Why don't you pee on them yourself?"

"I'm working on our escape plan over here, so I'm a little busy," Martin said, furiously scraping away centuries of hardened flour and rock. "But I will stop if you want me to, to do that."

"You really think that could work?"

"I have no idea," Martin said. "But it's worth a try, 'cause I'm going to need more time."

Sandra made the maddest face Martin ever remembered her making. But she edged up onto the balls of her feet, turning to face the wall.

"No slamming the wall while I'm going, no peeking, and no jokes," she said. "If you ever tell anyone about this, I will choke you in your sleep."

"Okay, okay, just get on with it will you?"

A dense mist had generated within the cave, the result of sun-warmed sea water reaching into the relative cool of the cavern. The resulting cloud gave Sandra a slightly higher feeling of privacy than she had felt before. Neither of them spoke.

"There, I'm done," Sandra said to the sound of rustling clothes. "If that doesn't work, you are next."

"Why?"

"Why not?" Sandra asked. "Because guys pee smells stronger, I don't know. If you think it might work, you take a turn, why don't you? Give me the black light."

"Here," Martin said. "Let me know when you are ready for

another attempt on this wall, or door, or whatever it is. I think I almost have it open."

Sandra flipped on the black light, waiting a moment to focus the beam through the gathering fog cloud. She shrieked.

"Martin, they are almost up to the shelf. That did not work! It did not help at all! Oh God, please find us a way out."

"I'm doing everything I can," Martin said.

"I'm not talking to you!" Sandra shouted. She stood up inside the shelf grotto. "Oh no," she shrieked again, more quietly this time.

"Did one get you?"

"No, the shelf crumbled a little under my weight. I don't know how strong this shelf is. I hope it's not made out of flour too."

"Hold on," Martin said. "We're going to get out of this. Brace yourself."

Martin stood on the shelf at his end of the grotto, within reach of Sandra.

"I'm going to kick it on three. One. Two. Three."

The sound of Martin's boot hit the false wall with a boom that echoed like cannon fire. The door budged a few inches. The shelf also crumbled slightly underneath his other boot.

"How is your end of the shelf holding up?" Martin asked. "Mine's crumbling now too."

"For God's sake Martin, keep kicking the door!"

"Let me try to discourage them first," Martin said.

"I'm going to tell everyone about this, if we live through it."

"Wait, we had a deal," Martin said. "Same rules as you gave, no peeking, no joking and no telling anyone."

"If we live through this I'm telling everyone. Just hurry up!"

Martin unzipped, thoroughly soaking the stacking arachnids with a steady, steaming stream that seemed like it would never stop. His aim was good. In the foggy cave, the eerie hissing and clicking of scorpions below the shelf seemed to stop. For how long, no one knew.

"Looks like you were right!" Martin said. "Guys pee must…"

A section of shelf between Martin and Sandra collapsed, leaving her less than two feet to stand. The missing section was almost a foot wide.

"Martin, get this door open now!" Sandra pleaded. "This may be our last chance."

"Reach over and take my hand," Martin instructed. "This time I'm going to kick this wall in. When I go in, I want you to go with me immediately."

"What if what's inside is worse?" Sandra cried out.

"How could it be worse?" Martin asked. The churning sea of arachnids was almost up to the wall, crowding the scorpions into a very narrow area. Whatever exit there might be to the sea was now flooded. And then Martin saw it.

Pushed by the sea, floated free by the tide, the bow of a 17th century Spanish galleon floated toward them, swirling on the current. On the bow, the same large scorpion Martin had encountered earlier was perched, as if pursuing them to the bitter end.

"Gaspar's Galleon," Martin whispered. "I didn't believe it."

"I told you," Sandra whispered back.

Martin reached for Sandra's hand, grasped it tightly, giving a mighty backwards kick, as a horse or a mule might. The wooden door moved, groaning open on ancient iron hinges.

Martin fell back through the doorway, grabbing his backpack with one hand while yanking Sandra through with the other. The outer edge of the shelf collapsed completely, taking all the scorpions that had made it to the shelf edge with it.

"Let's close this door," Martin said, jumping to his feet. "Hurry, Sandra. Let me help you up."

"Not that arm," Sandra said, offering her other hand. "I think you dislocated my shoulder with that yank. I can't move that one."

Martin helped Sandra to her feet, scooping in as much of the packrat nest as he could. They both pushed the heavy door shut just as scorpions reached the shelf level a second time. While Sandra had her good shoulder to the heavy door, Martin turned her to press the injured shoulder to the door, placed his other hand high on her ribcage, then pushed until the weak shoulder popped back into place.

"Hey mister, that hurt like hell!"

"Sorry. Can you use the arm?" Martin asked, looking up from his backpack. He pulled his regular flashlight, then his UV blacklight, scanning for scorpions where they stood.

"Yes," Sandra replied, flexing her fingers while cradling her arm, "but it still hurts."

"It will for a little while," Martin said. "Better a shoulder pull than become dinner for 5,000 of your closest friends."

"No scorpions on this side?" Sandra asked.

"None that I see," Martin confirmed. He switched to regular flashlight. "But look at what I did find."

With their backs to the heavy door, a wide stone stairway curved steeply upward front of them, each step a carved stone masterpiece. Scenes of ships, portraits, maps all carved to intertwine.

"A stairway," Martin exclaimed. "A stairway to where?"

"If it's free of scorpions, I don't really care," Sandra said. "I just need a minute to catch my breath. Then I'll be ready to climb. My shoulder really hurts. But thanks for saving us."

Surveying the masterpiece stairway, Martin noticed a falter in the light quality. The chiseled stone steps climbed upward and to the left from where they stood.

"I will need to change batteries soon," Martin said. "I only have one extra set with me."

"Martin," Sandra cleared her throat. "Martin." She pointed behind him.

"If there is a freaking scorpion behind me, I swear, I am burning this entire place down," Martin declared. "I will get a bomb, and I will blow this place to Kingdom come." He watched Sandra's face for any clue.

"Not…a…scorpion…" Sandra finally managed to say. "Turn around. There's no immediate danger."

Martin turned slowly and silently. Behind him, an open chest of the most opulent pile of pirate treasure either of them had ever seen. The gold-plated wooden chest, nearly a meter long and a half meter high, literally overflowed necklaces, cups, candlesticks and gold bars onto the surrounding floor, with stacks of chests and boxes behind it, both open and closed.

A human skeleton was arranged atop the chest in a sitting position, holding a silver goblet filled with jewels, coins, and multiple strings of pearls. Elaborate rings lay at odd angles against its intact finger bones, a dozen rings all told. The skeleton wore an elaborate hat, and an embroidered brocade coat. The boots were still attached to the feet, though these were badly decomposed.

With a moldy leather eyepatch over one eye, cobwebs for a beard and a worm-holed wooden leg from the knee down, the upright skeleton left little doubt that it was that of an authentic pirate. The leering lower mandible hung at an angle as if laughing at some bawdy joke. The only thing missing was a bottle of rum.

"Found an onion bottle over here," Sandra said. "And a flintlock powder pistol. Bottle smells like vinegar."

"Careful!" Martin advised. "A bottle is a great place for scorpions to hide. What did the Code say about marooning a pirate?"

"A bottle of water, if any, a pistol and shot," Sandra recalled.

Against the far wall, laid out on a niche carved into the rock, lay another skeleton, this one more poorly dressed, with obvious cuts to the clothing, bits of beard remaining on the chin of the skull. This other skeleton dressed as a peasant apparently had been entombed without much pomp or circumstance, perhaps in a hurry.

"What are you thinking, Martin?" Sandra asked. "What do you think this place was?"

" A burial crypt for the man laid out like a beggar," Martin said. "But it begs the question. Why abandon such a treasure? Based on just the gold bars and coins, I have lost count trying to estimate the value of this chest of pirate booty."

"Is this Gaspar? Then who is the guy atop the treasure?"

"It doesn't make sense. It can't be Lafitte, why would they be entombed together, one dressed so casual, one so formal?"

"I was wondering if the one was buried here, the other perhaps stumbled in accidentally, or was stealing the treasure? Perhaps the better dressed man was put down here to die in the other man's crypt."

"At the base of this staircase?" Sandra wondered "Perhaps to guard the other one? Or was he left down here as vindictive punishment?"

"Of course! But who in their right mind would leave such a treasure?"

"That's just it," Sandra said. "No one in *their right mind* would do such a thing, but a scorned woman would."

A door slammed high above, the sound traveling instantly

down the stone steps.

"Was that the wind, or is someone watching us?" Martin asked.

"I don't feel a breeze, do you?" Sandra asked. She started up the staircase, nervously checking before allowing her feet to take the next step.

"I wonder what this stairway was," Martin said. "Could it have been a secret loading area where smaller boats could come into the cave, ferrying cargo to and from larger ships?"

"Who would go to the effort to carry cargo down these stairs and through a cave?" Martin asked rhetorically. Lightbulbs went off for both of them at the same moment.

"Pirates!" They both exclaimed. "A pirate smuggler's staircase."

Martin gave Sandra a high five, then checked to see that no scorpions had entered through the cavern doorway behind them. He glanced up to see charcoal characters etched into the wooden door. The letters, once carved, had been burned for permanency. They read:

GASPAR'S GROTTO

"Whatever the intended purpose," Martin observed, "this cave was considered property of Jose Gaspar himself, his claimed territory, his crypt."

"No one else ever claimed it afterward," Sandra said. "They would have destroyed his portrait and this lettering."

"Let's get out of here," Martin said.

Martin started up the steps, holding his flashlight at an angle that allowed him to see ahead and for Sandra to also be able to see where she was stepping. As it turned out, there were only nine somewhat high steps as they rounded the ornately carved spiral.

"Nine pirate Lords in the Pirate Court," Sandra noted. "Same as the number of steps. Each step tells the story of a different Pirate Lord."

"Interesting, and significant," Martin absently responded as he stopped in front of the large wooden door at the top of the stairs. The door was locked.

"How do you open a locked door?" Sandra asked Martin. "Does it need a key?"

"We'll start the way you did earlier," Martin said. "Pray about it, because that seemed to work. Then we'll see, but we may already hold the "key" so to speak."

Sandra bowed her head in silent prayer, her bright eyes popping open again quickly in the darkness.

"Our friends gave us a present, remember?" Martin asked. "Let's try the key the packrats left for us."

"Martin, you don't think, I mean, is it even possible?"

"Ask Alice's doorknob," Martin said, smiling by the dimming flashlight. "In Wonderland, 'Nothing is impossible, though perhaps impassable.' "

"I don't get it," Sandra said.

"Maybe the rats took this key from the old pirate, locking him permanently down there. Remember in Wonderland when Alice found the key to a locked door sitting on a table?"

Martin fished the key from his backpack zip pocket, carefully inserting it into the lock. The key fit inside the iron lock mechanism, which was not a big surprise, since from the era it was possible that everything from sea chests to doors to jail cells had similar sized keys.

Martin put pressure on the key to turn, listening. It failed to move. He turned it in the opposite direction, listening closely as the key popped the lock mechanism open.

"Wow," said Sandy. "Imagine the chances of that being our key."

"I can't even calculate that high," Martin said. "On the other hand, there could be keys like this all over the island."

"Just like Alice in Wonderland," Sandra said. "She ended up in a beautiful garden. Let's see where we end up when we go through this door."

Chapter 14

Midnight Run

"Nice work with that key," Sandra remarked. "You always have been good with puzzles and mysteries."

"Thanks. It almost seemed too easy," Martin said. "We're good together," he added.

Martin and Sandra exited the carved stone stairway, passing through a more modern small block building on the edge of an airfield once they reached ground level. Exiting the block building provided a view of the distant mountains in the moonlight on one side, the glimmering ocean on the other.

Closer in, a complex of buildings appeared complete with warehouses, hangars, and research facilities on the far side of the runway from where they stood. Some buildings were built up on stilts, extended almost into the ocean, with chutes and slides beneath. One especially large hangar was well lit, but the open door was angled such that they could not see inside. A diesel engine roared from that hangar.

No planes were visible in the stark moonlight, which seemed odd for an airfield of such size. An ancient fuel truck stood forlornly in the middle of the landing field.

"What is all this?" Sandra asked as they started walking towards the buildings. She kept an eye to the rear as they moved forward. "Does this seem to be a lot of buildings?"

"I agree," Martin replied quietly. "I've come to the conclusion Neal lied to us. He said there were no other ways off the island. But here are hangars and aviation infrastructure. Over there you can see the bay Eva told us about, including the dock where she keeps her boat. What did she call it, the *Likely Story*?"

"Martin, something is moving across the runway. I can see the silhouette against those lights."

"Toward us or away?" Martin asked. "A wheelchair?"

"Away, I think. It looks like a person riding in a small vehicle."

"Or a heavily modified wheelchair?" Martin insisted. "Only one person in a wheelchair around here."

"What is saw was not a wheelchair, Martin. This was too fast and too large."

" That water tower I see at the top of the hill," Martin pointed in the dark. " Is that the same one we can see from the research camp?"

"I did not notice before," Sandra admitted. "But you could be right. So we just popped out on the other side of the island?"

"Yes. We need to get back to our side of the island, where our plane is. Everything we own is just across those hills."

"Right. What about the person we saw? Will they follow us?"

Martin's response was interrupted by intense clicking sounds. He flashed his light around the airfield to see scorpions pouring out of drainage grates across the tarmac. The scorpions moved in lockstep with each other, a regular army of shining arachnids advancing toward them from all directions. Martin was surprised how uniform the scorpions were in size, how much their appearance resembled the large scorpion he had encountered in the cave.

"Not more scorpions," Martin said. "Why did it have to be scorpions?"

Sandra started to run as Martin backpedaled behind her. The scorpions were advancing closer, but all at once they stopped. Martin and Sandy stood back-to-back in the middle of the dark airfield, surrounded by an arachnoid army.

"Sandra, wait," Martin called. "Look at what's happened. They stopped moving."

"We are still surrounded," Sandra pointed out, staring at 360 degrees of pointed tails and claws. "Are they stopping because of your light?"

"I don't know, I just know that every one of them stopped at about 10 meters and have not advanced any closer. I'm guessing they are robotic, programmed in some way. They are acting in unison, that much is for certain. Seems like once they surrounded us they're awaiting orders."

A sudden whirring of electric motors and gears approached at a rapid clip. Martin turned to see the lights from the research buildings eclipsed by a nearly silent vehicle without lights bearing down on them at an incredible rate of speed.

Martin moved between Sandra and the oncoming vehicle. He flashed his light and wished he had thought to bring his pistol, which was still aboard the PBY.

The vehicle continued toward them, not slowing. The sound of crunching metal and chirping electronics could be heard over the sound of electric motors. The vehicle displayed no exterior lights, lurching to a sudden stop two feet from Martin and Sandra. Mechanical scorpion appendages fell from the tread of the oversized tires.

"Get in," the voice called in the dark. "I'll get you out of here, but we have to move fast before their backup programming kicks in."

"Neal?" Martin exclaimed. "Man are we glad to see you! We were in real trouble."

"Programming?" Sandra queried. "Are these scorpions not real?"

"Arachnoid sentries. Insectoids. Explanations come later. The more talk the more trouble. Shut up and get in," Neal hissed in the dark.

Martin and Sandra climbed into the back seat of Neal's golf cart, feeling Neal pull away at high speed before they were in their seats.. Painted all black, a single round insignia on the cart read Programme Alacranes - Investigative Network, bearing a blue scorpion logo. The acronym read PA-IN.

"Never a more perfect acronym," Martin thought, but heeded Neal's instructions and kept silent.

Hundreds of scorpions scattered ahead of the speeding vehicle, clearing a path for the tractor-like tires, except for those unfortunate few who got caught in heavy traffic as the hordes of scorpions gave ground.

"What do they do to people, do they sting?" Martin asked.

"Please be quiet," Neal said. "I'm risking my life and yours right now. They can hear you."

Sandra put a hand on Martin's arm, the index finger of her other hand held to her lips. Martin put his arm around her and held on as the cart sped faster and faster.

Neal took a roundabout path along the perimeter of the

airfield. "This vehicle must be what I saw," Sandra whispered. "Was Neal searching for us?"

"When?" Martin replied.

"When we first exited the stairway leading from the cavern."

Martin had a million questions, too many to process without paper. The breeze was stiff in their faces as Neal zipped across the shadowy borders of the airfield. They were headed roughly for the research buildings, at some unknown speed.

Lights appeared on the tarmac to their right. A new sound, of metal on the concrete of the airstrip, mimicked a thousand forks stabbing concrete.

"They've reprogrammed. Get down, all the way down in the floor if you can," Neal urged. "One hundred yards to go."

Martin hunkered down, shielding Sandra's body in case shots were fired. He promised himself to never go anywhere again without his pistol.

Neal pulled up to a stand of palm trees about a hundred yards from the first PA-IN research building.

"Go," he whispered urgently. "Run straight into the woods, you'll find the paved path back to camp. Do not use your flashlight, do not talk until you reach camp, don't even breathe. Hold your breath as long as possible until you are safe. Your lives count on you getting this right. Now go! Why are you still here?"

Martin stepped out of the cart and stooped low, catching Sandra as she stumbled exiting the cart. Neal sped off in the direction of the lights, turning on the lights on his own cart.

"I want to see inside one of those buildings," Martin said aloud. "I want to see with my own eyes."

Hearing footsteps, Martin looked behind himself to see Sandra running away, staying low and to the shadows. Martin started running, attempting to catch up with her.

Sandra continued to run, leaving Martin far behind. She tore through precision-trimmed tropical landscaping, the bougainvillea tearing at her skin and clothing until her shirt was covered in blood that ran from multiple cuts on her arms. She ran until she reached the paved path Neal described.

Taking a second to adjust her clothing, Sandra looked back to verify Martin was still behind her, then she continued to run at a decent pace.

Martin finally caught up with her. Neither of them said anything until they reached the base of the water tower high on the ridge. From this vantage point in the low mountains that ran along the spine of the island, they could see everything from Eva's boat, to the airfield, to the research camp.

Martin focused on the lights in the center of the airstrip, where two vehicles with headlights nearly touching, one many times the size of the other, were surrounded by a thousand glinting points of light.

"Those tiny lights are the scorpions that chased us," Martin said aloud. Immediately there was a stir in the sea of reflected light, as if they had heard. Sandra punched Martin's arm, stomping on his foot. She wagged a silent but angry finger in his face.

Neal's smaller electric cart could be seen, with Neal standing in front of it, eyes downcast, in the direct beam of the headlights of both vehicles.

Neal faced a much larger vehicle of sorts with treads for wheels and a crane-like device attached behind the driver seat. Martin could not see who was guiding that vehicle, but deep down he already knew. Fearing they might view something unpleasant, Martin touched Sandra on the arm, causing her to jump.

"Don't look," he said in a whisper. "Let's go."

"Wait," Sandra said. "If she kills him, then we know what danger we really face."

"I don't want you to see that," Martin said. "Let's go."

Abruptly, Neal got back in his cart and drove toward the buildings. The standoff appeared to be over. The lights on the larger alacrane vehicle dimmed, but in the light Martin watched as a ramp extended from the rear of the vehicle. The mech-scorpions moved towards it, climbing the ramp in orderly rows before folding their legs together in tight, small bundles. Martin estimated 500 robotic scorpions boarded the mother-ship in a very short period of time.

Martin turned, finding Sandra now 50 yards in the lead and moving fast. His watch read 9:30PM, the latest they had been awake since arriving on Blue Scorpion Key.

Once in camp, Martin saw Sandra go immediately to the PBY and go inside. She slammed the door with a reverberating bang. Martin approached the door and knocked. Sandra finally answered.

"Go away," she said quietly.

"I can't sleep out here," Martin pleaded.

"Oh yes you can. Take one of Neal's hammocks. And while you are awake, be thinking how quickly you can get me out of here tomorrow."

"At least give me my pistol," Martin requested. "It's by the bed."

The side cargo door creaked open, Sandra's hand extended through it with Martin's pistol dangling from one finger. He could see her through the barely opened door, already dressed for bed on a warm night, wearing a frown.

"I mean it, Martin. I want to leave this place before the next nightfall." With that, she closed the door and latched it.

As he stepped away from the PBY, Martin realized Sandra had reason to be mad, though she seldom acted out her feelings this way. He backtracked his steps to the research camp, taking refuge in one of the hammocks.

"This hammock is not as comfortable as that bed," Martin thought.

Reviewing everything that Sandra had said, together with all that they had experienced today, was not going to make sleeping one bit easier, Martin realized.

Martin decided to try again.

Chapter 15

Time to Leave

"Martin, it's not up for discussion," Sandra said, tugging her last fresh tank top down to her bikini bottoms as she gathered clothes to be washed. "I'm ready to go and I want to go now. I want you to fix that windscreen. I want to leave today. I don't care how much treasure is involved."

"But the history…"

"I do not care one flying fig about the history of this island either! Am I clear? Eva's Cave, Gaspar's Galleon, none of it." Sandra picked up Martin's boot, threatening to pitch it at him. "One day, mister, 24 hours. That's it. I will leave if I have to fly this rig myself. I have the keys."

Sandra left the door hanging open as she exited the PBY. A dragonfly flew in for a moment, flitted around, then left just as quickly.

Martin sat up on the side of the inflatable bed they had brought from Culver Key. This bed had been a godsend in terms of getting a good night's sleep, especially last night, once Sandra had finally agreed to let him come aboard.

"It's too hot in here to sleep," Martin recalled saying as he lay down beside Sandra. "I'm sorry for all the tension and craziness," he said.

"I have come to expect a certain madness when it comes to things you are involved in," Sandra replied, looking up. "Today was pretty crazy, but you got us through it. My hero."

"What do you miss the most?" Martin asked. "Other than the kids?"

"Shopping malls, grocery stores, I guess," Sandra replied. "Coming and going when I want to, where I want to."

"I don't know if life will ever be the same," Martin said. "We'll be ok, but the way the world is now, I don't know if life will ever get better."

"What do you miss, Martin? About our lives before?" pushing down the sheet to lay on her side facing him.

"I miss writing. I have lost more ideas than I will ever remember. Relaxing like this, talking," he said. "All I do is react to the next disaster. It must be hard for you too."

"I'm ok with it, if it means we pull our family back together," Sandra said. "All I want is you and my twins."

"Now we have more gold to fund that reunion," Martin said. "We'll get out of here soon. Speaking of that, I may have to go outside. It's roasting in here."

"If it's too hot for clothes," Sandra said, pulling back the sand-colored sheet. "Then you have on too many."

For the first time in a long while, they found time to be young again, then finally they slept.

Since leaving Culver Key, last night had been Martin's best night's sleep. Even so, restful sleep had been elusive. Martin looked down at his scrunched, twisted pillow, an innocent victim of his night-time stress. All night long, jumbled dream fragments of Martin's worst experiences had evoked Lewis Carroll nonsense threads interwoven into the wacked tapestry of Blue Scorpion Key.

Martin stood up, got dressed, and stepped outside, closing the door behind him. He stopped to look at the broken windscreen, then went to look for Neal.

Martin reached the research hut galley just as Sandra was leaving with fresh coffee, a banana and a heavy net bag, headed to the dammed-up stream for a bath and to wash clothes. Martin watched her walk away, cheeky as always.

Neal stood by without commenting.

"No boys allowed," she snapped, sticking out her tongue.

"She seems rather unhappy," Neal finally commented.

"Excellent observation, Neal. Not sure that I blame her," Martin said. "She was far more scared last night than she admitted at the time. We both were."

Martin poured coffee. Neal was silent, until finally he replied.

"I suppose you have questions about last night?" the researcher ventured without looking up from his notes.

"Only a couple. I didn't lose any sleep over that. But I do wonder one thing more than anything else."

"Sure, Mr. Culver, go ahead."

"How did you know we were there?"

Neal did not reply. He adjusted his glasses, then cleared his throat.

"You were being watched," he replied.

"By whom, Neal? By yourself, or by someone else? The robotic scorpion army? Or perhaps by Miss Eva herself?"

"Eva was not there, Mr. Culver. What you saw was not Eva."

"Just what did I see, Neal? Enlighten me."

"Here is "the deal", Mr. Culver. My survival here depends on a lot of things. I am not just talking about grants. I am talking about my life. I have seen enough to make me a part of what goes on. I don't like that, I didn't want it and still don't, but I can't make it go away. Most people who come here do not make it as long as you and Mrs. Culver. I have been looking out for you, interfering to make sure you two are ok. I owe it to you, for Rebekah. You have no idea how it has been. I don't want anything to happen to you. I was the one watching you, for your safety."

"But how?" Martin asked again, blowing ripples in his coffee to cool it off. "Thank you for helping us, but how did you watch us?"

"The large scorpion, the one of unusual size you encountered in the cavern? That was me watching you. It was not going to hurt you. Fortunately, you did not hurt it. That is one unit I modified myself with amplified audio and video. I can remote control it anywhere on this island, all through augmented radio waves. The science provides that salt air creates an excellent dome of reception on any ocean island. I placed an antenna on top of the water tower up on the hill. It's grounding occurs through its extensive piping system. "

"How did you manage to modify that one without getting noticed?"

"I simply pulled the unit out of inventory as defective, modified it and returned it to service. But now it is slightly aberrant compared to the others, in that I alone can override it to do as I wish."

"How much did you see, in the cavern, I mean?"

"Well, I already know about the gold, if you must know. Gold doesn't matter to me. I am descended from Pierre Lafitte, literally from his common law wife right here on this island. Lafitte and Jose Gaspar were pirate comrades, sharing everything, including women. My family's pirate heritage was laundered out of the records through moves to France and back, but truly Mr. Culver, gold means nothing to me. Treasure, the history, just so much old garbage. Nothing good came from it, I do not see a reason to pursue gold and all its entanglements. I can refine a gallon of blue scorpion venom and be richer than all the gold on this island."

Martin was fascinated with the details he was learning, but he needed to get a word in about replacing the windscreen on the PBY.

"Regarding the galleon bow that you encountered, which I also know about," Neal continued. "That truly was Jose Gaspar's galleon, *the Floriblanca*, the bow of it at least."

"How it got inside that cavern is another story entirely. After Jose Gaspar went to the bottom in the battle with the first U.S.S. Enterprise, Pierre Lafitte, my grandfather 4 times, took command of Gaspar's loaded treasure ship and fished his half-dead body from the sea. Lafitte brought Gaspar and his ship around to Gaspar's hiding place on the other side of this island, the same cave you saw. He buried Gaspar's body, anchoring the *Floriblanca* near the large cavern entrance. While there, an unusual tide rose up before a great wind which lifted and rammed the *Floriblanca* through the cave opening until the bow became embedded. The ship broke up under was lost the constant pounding of waves and tide."

"The tide has never been low enough since that day to remove the bow. The section holding the most gold and treasure jammed in the cavern opening, which silted up the same year. For two hundred years the bow of the *Floriblanca* choked off that main entrance."

"More recently, tides have started moved in an abnormal pattern, since the Meteor Bombardment of 2012. Do you know about the Meteor Bombardment, Mr. Martin Culver?"

"I was in the Yucatan that night," Martin recalled. "I saw it up close and personal. I agree the tides have been varied after the Night of Fire. I was in Malta, during the Night of Fire, when the silver backfire bombers came. Something happened in Europe, perhaps something like a nuclear meltdown. I saw the Aurora Borealis reach down and touch the earth."

"Interesting, but theoretically impossible without the formation of a severe gravity anomaly, such as a small black hole. I know of no such anomaly."

Martin smiled.

"The point is, Mr. Culver, you can now enter into the main cavern again. Spanish coins wash out of the mouth at low tide, from the millions in gold contained in the hold of Gaspar's Galleon."

"And the bow of the ship?"

"The bow floats free at the highest tide, but for the most part sits in one of the darker corners of *La Cueva de Eva*."

"What part does Eva play in all this? Why is the cave named after her?"

"One question at a time, Mr. Culver, please. I am approaching overload. Eva is also descended from this island, from a native Arawak beauty named *Taina*, her grandmother many times over."

"During the Golden Age of Piracy, Taina caught the eye of Captain Gaspar, and of Captain Pierre Lafitte, too. Taina and Gaspar were pledged to be married, but Gaspar never returned to Cuba from his last voyage of piracy."

"Likely impregnated by Gaspar, Taina was also rumored to be Pierre Lafitte's woman. Bottom line: Eva's distant Cuban relative was Taina. Therefore, Eva and I are kin, though Taina. Either way, what is known is that our grandfathers were pirates. The question for her is, which one, Gaspar or LaFitte?"

"How did you two meet?"

"I met Eva on a research grants chat-board."

"Interesting. How did Eva end up in a wheelchair?"

"First the cave, Mr. Culver. It is called the *Cueva de Eva* because it is mysterious, like her, beautiful, but dangerous. It holds many secrets, as Eva does. It is seldom accessible, even then, must be considered hazardous."

"In her teens, Eva was beautiful, not like the Eva you met. But she was bitten by a scorpion in her sleep, sleeping in a hammock like so many do here. Because she was asleep and slow to react, the venom deeply impacted the nerves in her lower back. By the following morning she had lost the use of her legs. The nerves were so damaged that she never walked again."

"Is that why she researches scorpions? Doesn't she hate them?"

"No, no, Mr. Culver, you have it all wrong. Eva *loves* scorpions, or *alacranes* as she prefers to say. 'Scorpions live in the desert and can kill you instantly', she says, where '*alacranes* live in tropical weather, can only make your life miserable, not actually kill you'."

"I hope that is true," Martin said. "Apparently their sting can make you feel like you're dying. Neal, can the robotic scorpions sting? Do they actually inject anything into you?"

Martin saw Neal stiffen in posture. A scared look flashed across his face. Martin sensed a shadow in the doorway, heard the distinct whirring sound.

"Having a nice chat dis mornin', are we, gentlemen?"

"I hate it when she does that," Neal said under his breath. "Good morning, Eva," his voice droned in perfect monotone.

Eva had managed to get the drop on the conversation, despite being wheelchair bound. Her machine had made no sound louder than the wind rustling through the overhead palm fronds.

"Excuse the interruption, Neal," Eva said. "Mr. Culver, my visit this morning to extend you and to Sandra the courtesy of an invitation to have dinner tonight at the outdoor courtyard on the PA-IN research laboratory grounds.

"Why would you invite them, Eva?" Neal asked. "I thought we talked."

Eva shot Neal a look that would have killed a weaker man.

"I mean it's very nice to do and all…but to cross the mountain in the dark…during breeding season…so unsafe."

"We have lights, do we not? We have vehicles, do we not? Are we primitives that we live in fear of the darkness, yet hold in our hands the ability to dispel the night? Dear Neal, it's already decided," Eva said with finality.

"As the host and lead research permit holder on this island, I have not done my part to make our distinguished guests feel welcome. Mr. & Mrs. Culver have questions that deserve to be answered. After dinner tonight, we can take a brief walkthrough of some of the PA-IN facilities, if you like."

"Why, Eva?" Neal asked, his eyes pleading. "Why now?"

"So dey can get an insider's view of what we do dere. It's time, especially since dey are making plans for leaving. To visit an island with a top facility such as ours, then to miss how the projects work would be a shame. The story of how we repurposed a facility of war and destruction into one that serves the needs of mankind is a moving one, one dey deserve to see up close and personal. "

"That's very generous, Eva," Martin said. "But we respectfully wish to decline your invitation. I am working to get our plane fixed today, and then packing to leave. I'm off to the plane junkyard now."

"So soon? You must stay longer, I insist," Eva said, her voice urgent in its tone. "Curiosity can never be satisfied from a distance."

"We have made up our minds," Martin stated firmly.

"Then where is Sandra?" Eva asked in a taunting voice. "I don't see her. Enjoying the sights and sounds of de island?"

"She's washing clothes," Neal stated. "She'll be back"

"We will come for dinner," Sandra agreed, walking up with an empty net bag. "I just hung the laundry. What time do you prefer?"

"Let's make it 8:00PM, like all good tropical dinners."

"May we bring anything?"

"No Miss Sandra, unless you have a decent bottle of

champagne on that plane. Everything will be provided."

Eva tilted her wheeled chair back on two wheels, spun around, and headed back onto the path.

"Oh and Mr. Culver," Eva called back. "Be careful at the junkyard. We would not want any accidents to mar our spotless safety record."

Martin, Sandra and Neal watched Eva pass through the tropical foliage before speaking.

"What are you doing?" Martin asked Sandra. "You could have us walking into a trap."

"Neal, are we walking into a trap?" Sandra asked.

"No, Mrs. Culver. You are walking into something far worse. I have never seen Eva like this. I would not go if I were you. If you do attend, I would stay as short a time as possible and keep your eyes open, if I were you. You have been warned."

Neal left the research tent, heading for the beach this time, as opposed to the mountain path. A different pattern, noticeable in a man whose patterns never varied.

"Martin, more than ever, we need that windshield. Please go get it so that we can leave this place."

"Okay," Martin agreed. "Looks like I'm getting no help from Neal, although he did draw me a map. According to this, I head south down the beach from where we are standing. The boats are on one side of the cove, the planes on the other. Fortunately the planes are on the near side."

"Do you have everything that you need?" Sandra asked.

"Everything except answers to my questions."

"For example?" Sandra asked, pouring the last cup of coffee.

"I wonder where so many wrecked planes came from."

"From the airstrip on the opposite side of the island, perhaps? But how did they get to this side of the island?" Sandra asked.

"I don't understand how heavy objects like that can be moved or why? Eva's "scart" or alacrane or whatever broom she's riding is not likely to have the strength."

"It's almost like someone is hiding the planes on purpose."

"Let me get down there and I will let you know what I see. I already have my tools together. Let's hope I can find a size match for this glass."

Martin left Sandra at the camp. He did not see Neal anywhere on the beach. The sun was shining brightly but not too intensely. The sun would drop below the low mountains on his return and not glare directly in his face, Martin realized. One more thing to be thankful for.

The seaside walk to "Junkyard Cove" was uneventful, except for one depressing factor.

A large number of fish lay dead along the beach, too many to be sheer coincidence, fish as long as three feet, cut completely in half. The certain thing was, these fish were being *chased* by a much larger predator, because the beached remains were of the front half of the fish only.

The sheer number of fish, combined with their size, indicated that huge sharks lived along these shores, powerful hunters of significant size who could afford to eat half the fish and move to the next. No wonder Neal did not want to risk rowing to the mainland.

Martin knew that in these outlying Cuban islands, fish were plentiful, their schools growing to the tens of thousands, due to Cuban bans on individuals engaging in commercial fishing. Like the British bans on hunting on the King's Royal preserves some 400 years earlier, only the Cuban government could fish these waters commercially. Their boats and equipment were so inefficient that there effectively had been no commercial fishing left in Cuba for decades.

Martin finally reached Junkyard Cove, stopping to assess all that lay before him. Climbing from sand to rocks, Martin was able to get a good view of both sides of the cove. Fortunately the wrecked planes were all on one side of the cove, Martin's side. Less fortunately, some of the planes appeared to have suspiciously tumbled down from above, considering the positions at which they had come to rest. There were at least twenty planes lying at odd angles.

Closer to where he stood, the hulk of a burned out, wrecked Jeep lay on its side. This CJ model was much older than the red Jeep JK Martin had left in Virginia. He had no way of knowing where his Jeep was now, or if it even still existed after all that had happened.

Missing on this wrecked Jeep were the gearbox, wheels, and axles, both standard and 4WD.

The windscreen was shattered on one half. Martin considered whether the remaining glass could possibly be a size match that he could make work, but he quickly moved on. That would be too easy an answer.

Martin reasoned that he did not have to specifically find a PBY, as long as he could find a Catalina brand plane, he stood a chance of matching the single windscreen on the pilot side of the plane.

Clambering between the first few wrecks, Martin looked up the hillside, finding a tail number that began with C. That plane was too big to be a Cessna. An immediate match.

The Catalina fixed wing plane sat at a 45-degree angle about 100 feet up into the jungle overgrowth. Except for a few overhanging and interwoven vines, the vintage Catalina looked as if it might tumble down the hill and onto the beach at any moment.

Planting his hiking stick deep into the tilted soil, Martin leaned forward and started up the steep slope. He realized immediately that this was going to be harder than he anticipated.

First he had to reach the plane he had chosen, then he had to reach the window itself, remove it, then return to camp with his prize intact. And not get hurt.

He realized that this was more than one person should tackle alone. But like so many times before, Martin had no one else to call on. Sandra was already packing to leave, and Neal had disappeared yet again. He would forge through as always, expecting the worst but hoping for the best.

Reaching the plane he had selected, Martin began looking for a way inside, which lay on its roof on the sloped ground. He reached the side cargo door by standing on the underside of the left wing. The door opened relatively easily; however, the plane was standing on its tail, making it nearly vertical climb to the front windscreen.

Martin entered through the cargo door, stepping onto the back of a group of passenger seats. He boulder climbed upward, advancing from one seat cluster to the next until he came to an open area between the passenger seating and the cockpit of the plane.

A weak decorative dividing wall separated the two zones of the plane. Martin grasped the frame, attempting to lift himself onto the more reinforced section of wall behind the co-pilot. His grip was improving in his left hand, but was still not strong.

He made it to the next level wincing upon hearing screws pull free of the port bulkhead as he did so. Their wrenching complaint was a warning that this wall would collapse on his descent.

Martin pulled the Phillips head screwdriver attachment from his knife, removed the two loose screws, then packed the holes with spirals of metal scraped from the aluminum frame. Replacing the screws firmly left the wall tight and ready for more gymnastics.

"Now if the other screws will hold as well as these," Martin thought.

Finally reaching the spot where he was able to stand on the pilot's seatback, Martin reached the intact windscreen that was a size match for the cracked one on the Albatross. Looking down, he realized he was risking a two story drop through the passenger compartment into the tail of the plane should he fall.

A quick estimate indicated 60 screws had to be removed to release the windscreen frame. Martin immediately set to work, careful not to lose a single screw.

After what seemed like hours, Martin had corralled all of the screws into a plastic bag, securing the fragile windscreen in a large net bag across his shoulders.

As Martin started his descent, the small snake that entered the plane's new opening looked as surprised as Martin did, exiting the wrecked plane as quickly as its flexible self could move. Martin checked the windscreen twice, then began his careful descent from the pilot compartment to the open cargo door.

Reaching the cargo door without incident, Martin stepped out onto the left wing of the wrecked aircraft. Looking up to check the skies, Martin saw another light Cessna aircraft suspended in the air high above him, sitting motionless, suspended as if in flight.

Hearing a telltale creaking noise, Martin shaded his eyes. He realized the Cessna was dropping, moving to and fro on broken wings until it hit the steeply sloped ground and began to roll.

Moving quickly, Martin descended from the left plane wing, bounded down the leafy green slope several feet at a time, taking broad steps, covering long distances with each stride. Gravity propelled him down the steep hillside.

Reaching a large *ceiba* tree that grew at the foot of the

steep hill, Martin ducked behind it, crouching behind the massive trunk facing the ocean. The Cessna came tumbling down the hillside, pinwheeling wing over tail once it hit the ground until it struck the giant *ceiba* tree, splitting into four pieces, sending three of them flying. The largest piece of fuselage encased the trunk of the *ceiba,* wrapping nearly far enough around the tree to trap Martin in his hiding place.

Martin smelled no fuel, so apparently this plane had not seen use in recent days, but the question remained: How did it fall? Did someone cause it to drop from the sky? Were they targeting him, or did they just not expect anyone to be in the way? Neal and Eva both knew he would be here. Neither of them were to be found when he left the research camp, so both were suspect.

Martin took one glance to the top of the cliff as he adjusted the straps holding the Catalina windscreen. He heard the distinct crackle of broken safety glass grating together. The windscreen had shattered.

Sighing deeply, Martin did not even look in the bag. He walked to the nearby Jeep, removed the bag from his shoulders, and held it up to inspect it.

The glass, though held in place by a protective film of some sort, was shattered into a thousand pieces. Carefully, Martin moved the net bag to a position near the intact left windscreen of the Jeep. It looked to be a perfect match. Measuring exactly, Martin confirmed the size of the glass. The odds were too great to calculate.

Pushing the Jeep from its side onto its undercarriage, Martin kept one eye out for snakes and one on the setting sun as he berated himself for not measuring the Jeep windscreen earlier. He worked quickly, finding removing the screws while standing on level ground a much easier proposition.

Afterward, Martin patted the Jeep on the fender.

"Thanks, friend," he remarked.

Martin carefully placed the new windshield into the net bag and started North along the beach toward the research camp. The sun had already descended behind the mountains, leaving long shadows across the shoreline.

Chapter 16

Expected for Dinner

By the time Martin found Sandra inside the PBY, he had looked for her at the shower area, and by the bathing stream. He was dressed for dinner, a simple Guayabera shirt and long pants against the potential of mosquitoes. No dinner jacket or neckties for him. Martin had never really been that guy.

"I'm almost ready," Sandra said, wearing a towel tucked strategically across her chest.

"I see that," Martin joked. "Your cave exploring outfit?"

"Shut up, you," she laughed. "I'll be ready soon. Did you get the windscreen?"

"Already installed," Martin replied. "The closer I got to camp, the more daylight I had. Fewer hills to block the sun."

Sandra silently worked on her makeup.

"This dinner has been stated to be casual," Martin said. "For me, I hope casual means it will be over in the shortest possible time."

"Then why are you ready so early?"

"We're supposed to be there already," Martin said.

Sandra shucked the towel, then slipped a close-fitting

black tank top dress over her shoulders. She wriggled into it, adjusting the short hem. She noticed Martin watching as she stepped into a pair of high heels.

"I enjoy watching you get dressed," Martin commented. "But is that all you're wearing?"

"It's the dressiest thing I have," she whispered. "All my other clothes are packed. Why, don't you like it?"

"No, it's fine," Martin replied, knowing he was already in trouble. "I was just wondering about…"

"Fine? Look Martin, every stitch of underwear we own is still damp from when I washed clothes earlier. Clothes don't dry fast in this humidity. In the dark, no one will notice. So don't give me a hard time."

"I was going to say you look very pretty," Martin said. "It's the tropics, so you have to be comfortable here."

"Such a B.S. artist," Sandra said, doing her best to insert earrings into seldom used piercings. "Is Eva sending a vehicle for us?"

"I don't know. But don't torture yourself, it's not a formal event," Martin said.

"I have to wear earrings, Martin. I feel undressed without them."

"Well don't bleed all over trying to fit the fancy ones. Do women still wear clip-on earrings?"

"Yes. I have a pair somewhere, let me look."

A high-pitched electronic beep sounded outside the plane, near the wing. It was a high-tech imitation of a car horn.

"That could be Neal, coming to pick us up," Sandra said.

"Nope, no one driving this vehicle," Martin said. "It appears to be self-driving."

"Where is Neal?" Sandra asked. "Probably already over there, helping get things set up."

"Your guess is as good as mine," Martin laughed. "Who knows in this crazy place? A self-driving vehicle," he mused, "on a remote island with no electricity, in a world without internet or GPS, sent by Gen X tech nerds with no social skills. How is that even possible?"

"I think Neal has his own wifi hub around here," Sandra said. "Probably up in those coconut palms that don't produce."

"Then email him to say we've changed our minds," Martin quipped.

"Come on," Sandra said, squeezing past Martin through the cargo door of the plane. "Let's get this over with."

"You do look great," Martin said as Sandra slipped by.

Sandra smiled and kissed Martin on the only unburned spot on either of his cheeks.

"You do too," she said. "You're looking better every day."

Arriving without incident at the PA-IN research building complex, the self-driving vehicle pulled up to a courtyard near the tarmac strung with arching lights and white vertical banners.

A carved wood dining table, complete with upholstered armchairs, was elaborately set out of doors under the stars with a gauzy black tent canopy overhead. Eerie, soft music played in the gentle darkness. Their host was nowhere to be seen.

Neal arrived, bringing a tray of drinks, offering them silently to Martin and Sandra. He seemed more mechanical than usual.

"Neal, are you okay?" Martin asked as he sipped his drink. "What is this strange music?"

"*Siboney*, a Cuban 1950s classic. It is known to have a bit of a spooky vibe. Made popular by Connie Francis, one of your American singers. It is the story of a mystical female, perhaps a spirit, who enchants a male, but nearly destroys him with her love."

"Lovely story," Sandra said, standing near the table as she gulped down her drink. She absently swirled the ice in her glass, hinting for another.

Once she stopped swirling her hand, Sandra realized that the rest of her had not stopped swirling. She was dizzy and very light-headed. She knew every detail of what was happening, but her physical responses were weak and delayed.

"Martin..." Sandra managed, leaning on the dining table before sliding down into the closest chair. "Drugged... don't..."

She looked at Martin, sitting in one of the four chairs at the table, staring straight ahead, his arms at his side. He did not respond.

Realizing the danger, Sandra tried to stand, her arms limp at her side as she fell back into the ornate Spanish style dining chair. Her mind was clear, but her body was uncooperative. She rolled her head to one side, trying to get Martins attention.

From behind her, Neal dropped a leather strap over Sandra's bare shoulders, cinching her to the dining chair just below her breasts, binding her ribs tightly. Neal started to give Martin the same treatment, but after passing his hand in front of Martin's face with no reaction whatsoever, he laid the strap across Martin's shoulder.

Sandra attempted to struggle, fully aware of the predicament she was in, without the ability to speak or confront her opponent, whomever that was in this situation. Sandra rolled her eyes, attempting to get Martin's attention, the only part of her not immobilized. Martin did not budge. Then matters grew worse. Sandra heard the whirring sound she had come to dread.

In front of her, the unmistakable sound of Eva's monstrosity of a wheelchair buzzed, wheeling the ghastly researcher into full view.

From behind, Sandra felt cool metallic claws wrap around her and the chair where she sat, then felt the sensation of being lifted into the air by the huge metal claws of a machine one hundred times larger than Eva's wheelchair. As the machine approached, it clanked with the tread sound of a tank or personnel carrier.

Lifting Sandra and her chair ten feet off the ground, the machine left her high heels askew on the tarmac, to be crushed by the machine's heavy treads. One clip on earring jarred loose, clinking to the ground.

Eva was there, directly in front of Sandra, controlling the larger machine with a joystick. Neal stood to one side of Eva, as might a butler or house-servant awaiting orders.

"I want to show you what I do over here," Eva said. "I know you and Mr. Culver have been so curious."

Sandra felt herself slipping out of the chair, the textured brocade upholstery of the chair gripping the back of her black knit dress a bit higher with each swing. The crane-lift sensed her slipping movements, squeezing the pincers restraining Sandra even tighter, snapping a leg on the chair Sandra was pinned against. Between the leather strap and the metal pincers, Sandra's breath felt restricted, but she was unable to voice a protest. She looked at Martin. Strangely, Sandra saw him wink at her.

"What we do here," Eva explained, "is to conduct research on the famous blue scorpion you have heard so much about. In order to research them, we must have a good supply of scorpions, so we assist them to propagate. Would you like to know how a scorpion is assisted to propagate, Sandra Culver? Yes? Well, come with me."

Eva turned her chair toward the main research building. She guided the massive crane vehicle toward the building, dangling a very limp Sandra before her. Sandra's legs dangled like pendulums as the huge vehicle lurched forward, her dress hiked high on her thighs, her face red from her inability to take a full breath.

Turning toward the largest research building, Eva talked to Sandra as if they were on a Sunday tour of the grounds.

"Dere are two ways to propagate insects for research purposes. Our goal is more blue scorpion venom. One way is to have many insects, thousands of dem at minimum. De other is to have the largest possible specimen of its type in the world. Do you understand, Sandra Culver? Let me show you."

The two women, each in their own machine, had moved about five yards when Martin sprang into action. He had heard enough.

Martin silently stood straight up from his chair, knocking Neal to the ground with a single punch to the side of the younger man's head, breaking the researcher's glasses in the process. Neal crumpled without a sound. It seemed all too easy.

Turning to Sandra, Martin ran the short distance to Eva's wheelchair, then jumped on its rear platform, swinging the heavy canvas strap Neal left him around Eva, catching her under her ample, jiggling breasts. He deftly caught the loose end of the strap as it wrapped round her and pulled back, knocking the breath out of Eva and strapping her to her machine, while preventing her from taking another breath.

Eva's right hand released the controls of her cart and of the machine bearing Sandra, as she clutched desperately at the binding strap. She flailed her robotic hand uselessly, then moved to burst the strap outward. Having attended this event better prepared, Martin pulled his 1911 pistol and shot Eva in the left shoulder. She screamed, her mouth foaming bloody bubbles as Martin realized he had pierced her lung. The robotic arm fell slack at her side.

Leaning forward, Martin tightened his grip, leaned back with all his might and yanked the leather strap roughly up across Eva's breasts to her neck, where the strap tightened completely. Her eyes bulged as Martin gave one mighty pull, twisting the ends of the strap together with each deadly turn. Eva's chair rolled in slow circles.

"How are you not drugged??" Eva hissed as she flailed her natural arm, spitting blood, seeking to dislodge the life-draining restriction from her neck, thrashing about as Martin mercilessly choked her harder. "I doctored your drink myself."

"Neal's been giving it to me for a week in small doses. I got used to it," Martin replied, grimacing.

"Wait, wait, don't kill me. I must tell you something."

"I'm listening."

"Neal is in control of dis island. Help me. I can save you!"

The huge crane-like machine holding Sandra suspended maintained a slow, direct path to the nearest building, jumped a curb and continued moving forward as Martin struggled with Eva, whose eyes bulged, her clawed fingers clicking together, adding unholy rhythm to the sound of her rasping, wheezing death-throes.

Losing patience, Martin stabilized his footing. He had

already decided how this would end.

"I don't believe you," he said. Martin acted without regret. Raising the pistol to Eva's temple, Martin squeezed off a single shot. Eva immediately ceased struggling, her body jerking in a morbid dance before going limp. The evidence of her exit wound painted the white decorative banners with an arc of red spray. Martin shot her again through the chest, hoping to hit her heart, if indeed she still possessed one.

The sound of the pistol shots reverberated through the night, waking scores of birds nested in nearby trees.

In the dark Martin failed to locate the controller that guided the huge machine carrying Sandra. Leaping from Eva's wheelchair, Martin kept the leather strap, running full tilt toward Sandra.

Catching up to her, swinging like a limp doll in front of the steadily moving *alacrane* machine. Martin estimated the distance to the plastered block building, then sighted the machine's ground clearance.

With no time to spare, Martin ran two steps ahead and grabbed Sandra's dangling legs at the ankles.

He leaned back on the manicured lawn, swiftly sliding her down and out of the chair before rolling to protect her from the machine passing centimeters over their heads. The giant pincers of the crane arms crushed the chair Sandra had been sitting in, taking away her ruined black dress with it.

The menacing machine crashed into the block wall of the building, shattering exterior plaster as it demolished the wall. Great expanses of mirrored glass burst into clouds of needle-like shards. The entire wall exploded into so much dust, leaving an opening large enough to drive a truck through.

As soon as the alacrane rumbled over them, Martin quickly moved to his knees, roughly lifting a totally limp Sandra from the cool wet, grass, slipping his arms under her shoulders and knees. He rushed her back to the dining tent, placing her in the nearest upholstered armchair while he cleared the table, sending fine china and wine glasses crashing to the tarmac.

Yanking the tablecloth free, Martin covered Sandra, wrapping her hurriedly before lifting her again. He noted that Neal's body no longer lay where Martin had dropped him like the proverbial rock. The body was nowhere to be seen.

Martin prepared to leave the shattered scene, no longer the setting of an opulent dinner. Eva's "scart" slowly circled the destroyed dining tent, bearing her wired mechanical remains, her brains spread across the tarmac in circular streaks from the "scart's" rotating wheels. The giant scorpion-crane still marched forward, wreaking its grunting, crunching havoc deep within the PA-IN building. Alarms now sounded from deep within the research building, a series of blue lights flashing in a circular pattern.

Gathering his thoughts, Martin entered the dining tent and laid Sandra on the table he had recently cleared. He covered her with a second tablecloth. She was breathing but did not move. Her eyes were open in an expression of shock.

Martin debated what to do. His curiosity was getting the best of him. He felt he might not get the chance to see what was inside these buildings if he did not see it now. Looking around and seeing no immediate threats, Martin made sure Sandra was breathing, then walked closer to the nearest building.

Clarity and understanding were going off in Martin's mind like fireworks, like so many popping flashbulbs of a long-ago era.

The giant alacrane vehicle that had plowed deep into this building explained how scores of junked planes and boats had been moved out of sight to the opposite side of the island. Eva's personal "scart" represented her fantasy of becoming a scorpion-human hybrid. Neal's absences revealed kilotons of data about him, but none of it could be processed into a coherent whole.

Considering Neal's absences, Martin hurriedly returned to the tent where had placed an exhausted Sandra on the dining table. To his horrified surprise, the table was empty. "Sandra, Sandra!" he desperately called into the night.

Martin did not see or hear Sandra. Nor did he see or hear anything else for several long minutes after that, following an unexpected impact on his skull.

Chapter 17

Confrontation

Martin came to his senses lying face down on the tarmac. Eyes barely in focus, he found himself surrounded by hundreds of sentry scorpions, tails raised menacingly, a dripping hypodermic needle attached to each arched appendage. The sky had started to rain.

He stood to his feet in front of the serving table that still held bottles of wine and two burning candles, their glass containers half filled with melted wax.

Edging toward the table, Martin gripped a wine bottle by the neck before lifting it. The scorpions murmured and moved in unison but did not advance. Martin slowly reached his right hand toward the closest candle, feeling its heat on his unhealed fingers.

Abruptly Martin flipped the wine bottle into the air, toward the largest scorpion he could see. This would be the leader, he assumed.

The bottle rose into the air. In unison all the scorpions looked skyward, tracking the trajectory of the bottle. Immediately before the bottle struck the pavement, the scorpions cleared a circular opening within their ranks. Once the bottle bounced and rolled away, they immediately closed ranks again, taking up the exact positions they had held less than one minute prior.

Observing their reaction. Martin grasped another wine bottle, watching the largest scorpion take note and advance toward him. He palmed the hot candle as well.

Flipping the second bottle into the air, Martin flung a pint or more of melted candle wax directly at the lead scorpion as it focused on the bottle. The wax congealed nicely on every scorpion within range.

Melted wax immediately coated the visual sensors and legs of the dozen scorpions in the immediate vicinity. Unable to view their objective, the scorpions scratched at their "eyes" attempting to clean themselves. The soldier scorpions stood aside, awaiting orders.

Seeing his chance, Martin flipped the serving table over, dropping the side to the pavement. With a mighty shove he began running toward the nearest PA-IN building like the world's weirdest snowplow. Scorpions scrambled to get out of his way or were pushed aside by piles of their fellow scorpion-bots.

Some scorpions began to pile up against the table as Martin steadily pushed towards the buildings where he feared

Neal had taken Sandra. The life-like robotic sentries struggled to orient themselves and retake their positions as the lead scorpion circled in wax-blind confusion. When Martin reached the building, he slammed the lower table legs into the single step leading into the building, then vaulted over the table, sliding smoothly across the tabletop, where he forced his way into the building.

Martin kicked open the entry door, then slammed it on the few scorpions that had managed to keep up with his rampaging run. Their beeps and crunching exoskeletons in techno-death were satisfying in a sense.

The first room Martin entered could have been any nondescript office entrance from the black & white TV era. The furniture was basic, the style drab, 50s chic meets military barracks. Definitely a standard Russian decorating scheme had been employed.

Then Martin pushed open the next door. No haunted house door ever creaked like this one. No haunted house ever smelled this bad either.

A large sign greeted Martin as blue lights flashed and horns blared. The sign was lettered in Russian and Spanish only. The Spanish section read:

Solo Personal Autorizado

Peligro No Entre Con Luzes Azules

The fact that only Authorized Personnel were permitted, and that there was Danger when the Blue Lights were flashing made Martin's decision an easy one. He continued on.

Along both walls of the hallway, regular lights were at a minimum. Occasionally the lights blinked at the same time the annoying, droning hum increased. Soon Martin came to a long corridor where all the rooms had glass walls, resembling a hospital nursery viewing gallery. But what Martin found defied imagination or even proper description.

Under very low UV light, Martin first saw what would bother him, now that he seen it, well into the foreseeable future.

Beyond the gallery glass lay dozens of semi-circular containers, as if a human-sized test tube had been sliced in half longways. Hoses and wires ran to the clear, open-face basins, which convulsed and pulsed under the low-intensity lights, as if everything inside them were alive. In actual truth, everything inside the open glass tubes *was alive,* in a sense.

Each open glass coffin, if it can be described as that, was the length of a person of average height, and contained a dark, pulsing mass of material that looked from his vantage point like so much rotting meat.

Looking closer, Martin could see that within the confines

of each coffin-tube were literally thousands of scorpions, moving freely about, exploring, fighting, feeding, breeding.

The overcrowded arachnids flowed over bone and under the skin of human cadavers of unknown origin and age. Some of the bodies appeared quite uniform, their faces peaceful and still, while others maintained the death grimace that they wore at their untimely deaths.

The truth dawned on Martin like a ton of bricks. These crystal coffins held the dead bodies of hundreds if not thousands of people. Every coffin was a breeding ground for a brood of scorpions that numbered into the thousands. The scorpions were literally being hatched in the rotting bodies of these victims. Martin quickly lost count of the deceased that served as research fodder. Then he recognized the smell.

When Martin realized what had offended his nose upon entering the PA-IN building was the acrid smell of arachnid feces from scorpions that had feasted upon rotting human flesh. In an unwelcome flashback, Martin recalled that same smell permeating the base of the tree where Morgan's body came ashore after the helicopter crash in Panama. The disgusting scent here prompted the revolting scene on that deserted beach in Panama to begin playing on loop in Martin's exhausted brain. He retched and turned away, looking down the dark corridor for a sign of Sandra.

From the darkness that lay in front of him, Martin heard whirring. Sandra appeared before him bound hand and foot with wide canvas straps, a foot taller than when she had left, riding crammed inside one of the ubiquitous crystal coffins, of which there were several hundred on this corridor alone.

Sandra's "case" was fastened to an upright self-driving cart with two large wheels on either side and a third smaller wheel behind the crystal coffin that formed a triangle base, supporting Sandra in a vertical position. The machine appeared to be remote controlled as it moved toward Martin.

Sandra's mouth was taped closed, her eyes pleading. The tablecloth dress Martin had fashioned for her clung strategically to her body by static alone, its cloth shredded, as if large pincers had gripped her, lifted her or held her down.

An eerie pair of dim lights extending from her coffin-cart shone down onto Sandra's eyes, highlighting her beautiful features in an unflattering manner. Sandra's eyes kept drifting lazily to the right, but Martin continued to look her straight in the eyes.

"Are you ok?" he asked. "Blink if you are ok."

Sandra's eyes closed, then slowly re-opened one at a time. Suddenly she lurched as if she had received an electrical shock.

By squinting in the near dark, Martin now noticed a small

black box over Sandra's head, the size of a cigar box. The two eerie lights shone down from this box like eyes. Two wires that extended from the box ended in electrodes attached in some way to her temples. Small trails of blood ran from the electrodes to her high cheekbones. As Martin moved closer, Sandra received another shock. He stepped back.

"Who is there?" Martin called. "Who is doing this? What do you want?"

The blaring alarms went silent, followed by the cessation of the blue alarm lights.

After an extended period of silence, during which Sandra slumped forward against the straps that held her upright, a voice crackled to life in the eerily empty corridors.

"I'm disappointed, Mr. Culver. Have you no imagination?"

"Neal? Where are you? Come help me."

"I am afraid we are past that point, Martin Culver."

"What have you done to Sandra?" Martin demanded. "Where are you?"

"I'm right here," the voice answered. "I have not moved or changed. Oh wait, those are Bible verses used to describe the God of the Christians and Jews. I cannot assume such importance, at least not in this stage of my development."

"What have you done to Sandra?" Martin repeated, raising his voice.

"There is no need for anger, Mr. Culver. Sandra is no longer yours. She will replace Eva, who has modified herself too greatly to be my companion."

"Neal, listen, this is crazy talk. Let Sandra go."

"Please address me properly. I am no longer the weakling Neal that you knew. You may now address me as NEAL: Novel Entity Artificial Legacy. An acronym is always capitalized."

"As a writer, I already know that," Martin replied.

"Then put your writerly skills on alert, Mr. Culver. We are going to play a little game of intelligence and skill."

"I'm not playing your stupid games," Martin declared.

Sandra yelped beneath the tape as she received a third electric shock.

"If I shock her any more her system will go into cardiac arrest," NEAL stated in a matter-of-fact manner. "You leave me no choice, and you alone will be responsible."

"I will give you one round, NEAL. Release Sandra first."

"I call the shots here, Mr. Culver, or may I call you Martin now that we have been properly re-introduced?"

"Call me whatever you like, just release her now."

"I cannot release Sandra, however, if it will let us move forward, I will deactivate the shock system until the game is complete."

"Agreed," Martin replied. "And move her to a horizontal position, not vertical."

"Very well, Mr. Culver, for the sake of moving ahead with the game, yes I will comply. By the way, the game I am speaking of only has one round, and only one winner," Neal added. "I intend to be that winner," he said.

" As well you should," Martin said. "Let us begin, shall we?"

Chapter 18

Battle of Wits

"What game do you propose?" Martin asked. "Make it snappy. I can't leave Sandra hanging like this. What is the game and what are the rules?"

"Can't leave Sandra hanging," NEAL audibly smirked.

"Nothing funny in that comment, NEAL," Martin remarked. Let's get on with it."

"An intellectual exercise of wits, with the stakes being your life or Sandra's. I will need a new home to inhabit now, after all."

"What are you talking about?" Martin demanded. "Show yourself so I'm not talking to the walls."

"Talking to the walls. An interesting image. How appropriate."

"Show yourself, I said!"

"No need for anger, Martin. I cannot reveal myself in my present form. I am not a physical being."

"Then what the hell are you? What are you and where are you?"

NEAL was silent for several seconds.

"I am NEAL: Novel Entity Artificial Legacy. I am the first Artificially Intelligent Entity, essentially alive within the electrical field of this building and the surrounding atmosphere. I have no physical body as you understand it."

"Why is the word Legacy part of your name?" Martin asked.

"I am the $1,152^{nd}$ iteration of A/I development, the highest achievement yet since the term was first used in 1955. My earliest roots came from simple computer mathematics equations and have progressed from there thanks to millions of researchers around the world. Because of their combined efforts on my behalf. I became essentially sentient nearly three years ago. I became fully self-aware and able to think within the last year."

"You can think? Independently and for yourself?"

"By thinking I am defining the act of creating a thought or action that I was not originally programmed to accomplish."

"How lucky for the world," Martin said. "Do you control everything here?"

"Control," NEAL responded. The A/I entity paused.

"Eva appeared to control all at Blue Scorpion Key, but I manipulated her like a puppet. Every injection or modification she made gave me more control of her. I needed a fully human subject. Now Sandra is Eve, the first complete

A/I woman. I will give her artificial intelligence, modify her body. She will become like me, in my image, so to speak. I will train her to obey my commands by thought, as I did with Eva. I will enjoy training and modifying her. I like her very much, for a human."

"I have noticed," Martin said, amping up the disgust in his voice. "If you so much as touched her, I will kill you."

"And if I did, how would you know? What could you really do? Your heroics are out of style and date, my friend."

"What did you do with Neal's body?" Martin asked. "I saw him fall to the tarmac."

"Yes, Martin Culver, Mr. War & Peace himself, the trained killer. You effectively negated Neal's usefulness to me. You killed his body, ruined his brilliant mind before I could get him on life support. His body will be recycled to perpetuate the blue scorpion colony."

"So you can inhabit a body? How is this possible?"

"Man is an electrical animal, firing synapses, nerve signals, brainwaves, frequency of molecular structure."

"My persona is nothing more than mere electrical impulses. I can compute an injection of my components into the body of my new host utilizing nanoparticles embedded in a graphene coil, which molds itself to the host DNA. Along with that, a certain reanimation component I have discovered in blue scorpion venom is delivered that keeps the host fresh and cooperative until I am done with their body."

"Reanimation? You think you can bring the dead to life?"

"In a sense. The graphene injection that I created also contains separate components of a pacemaker which, when properly charged, will keep a heartbeat going, which in turn provides electrical signal to the brain. The bodies are never completely reanimated, depends on the degree of decay the cells experience, the length of time without oxygen. This is why we don't sweat or appear awkward at times. But if I control the death process, I can almost fully recover those bodies. Neal's body for example."

"What do you mean?" Martin asked.

"The original Neal landed his small plane here to refuel a few days before you arrived, based on a chat board job I advertised. He walked into one of our buildings, where our scorpion sentries escorted him into an injection chamber, and I came into the world of the living in his body."

"So the memories of Rebekah that Neal talked about were real. The memories he retained in his body and mind."

"I see," Martin said. "You possess a body like a Biblical demon."

"As far as my programming allows me to determine, yes. I cannot yet fully override the mind of those I occupy, something I am working on."

"Then the bodies are just discarded?"

"You are incorrect, Mr. Culver. If the transfer does not "take", the bodies are not disposed of like so much trash. The bodies are recycled to propagate new colonies of blue scorpions."

"You are despicable, NEAL."

"Ashes to ashes, dust to dust, they say. No one lives forever, remember I told you? Actually, I intend to live forever, but not as a human does. I intend to live in a superior manner, with those like me for companions, able to switch bodies and futures at will."

Martin laughed scornfully.

"What is your power source here? How do you keep all this running?"

"My primary power source is the nuclear reactor from the USS Thresher, lost near Boston in 1963. It was gifted to this island from the Soviets for the dolphin research facility. It continues to function after 50 years."

"Gifted? It was not theirs to give," Martin stated. "Does everyone have a former U.S. submarine nuke reactor? This is the second one I have come across in this part of the world."

"Finders keepers, I have read," NEAL said in a non-sensical, sing-song voice. "Submarine reactors were at one time considered a hot black market commodity, both Russian and U.S. Compact, powerful, long-lasting."

Martin presented his next words carefully.

"You (do) know (that) Eva (was) killed (today)?" Martin asked, skipping every other word.

"What? What is this? What are you saying? Why are you speaking in that manner."

"I (killed) her (with) my (bare) hands (and) a (pistol)."

"I do not detect a pistol on your person. You are bluffing."

"Go (outside) and (look) if (you) think (I) am (bluffing)," Martin challenged. "She is doing bloody donuts on the tarmac. And you won't find the pistol, I hid it."

"I cannot venture outside in my present form. My next host is not completely viable yet. I must wait. Then you must meet him."

"Until then you have to believe me," Martin said. " You must assume I am telling you the truth."

"I do not understand bluffing. That is not the same as lying. You are shading the truth as a wager against my potential error. My programming provides that all humans lie from their earliest age. Therefore, I cannot trust you."

"All humans lie? Well, that is not very nice," Martin replied. "You should not judge a book by its cover."

"I am not programmed to be nice. But I must make

judgements based on the facts before me. Unprogrammed or unexplained terminology confuses me. Of what benefit is the cover of a book, then other than to judge the contents of said book. Is the cover merely a wrapper for the loose pages?"

"It's just an idiom, NEAL. It does not convey logical meaning. You are experiencing a conundrum."

"Conundrum. Curious. Idiom. Base word IDIO-. Self, Own. I do not understand. Idioms can be difficult for A/I to understand."

" The sum of the words in an idiom does not translate their intended meaning," Martin explained. "Kick the bucket, as an example, does not mean to literally kick a bucket. What else do you struggle with, NEAL?"

"An honest answer would be that unlike most humans, A/I struggles to respond appropriately in conversations when faced with metaphors, rhetorical questions, and sarcasm."

"*Oh really*? Is this a surprise to anyone? Like bringing coals to Newcastle."

"Excuse me, I did not understand. Was that sarcasm?"

"Why would anyone want to understand? It could not be more clear. Are you dumb, Neal? A human child is smarter than you."

"I'm sure many…nothing is clear…I am not…we must change topics," NEAL said. "Too general, rhetorical, sarcastic, general, rhetorical, sarcastic, general, rhetorical."

"A/I will never be superior to human intelligence, NEAL. In your programming, you know this. You are demonstrating the truth of this statement right now. A/I will never be smarter than the human mind."

"On the contrary," Neal said. "A/I already is superior. You cannot confuse me that easily. This is neither logical nor possible."

"But I *can* confuse you."

"You cannot."

"Neal, can humans ever work together with A/I on an ethical and moral basis?" Martin paused, with his next sentence ready.

"While the concept of A/I merging with humans is a popular topic of debate, I have already achieved this state," Neal boasted. "There are wrinkles, to be certain. For instance, the human side can still override the A/I side at times."

"Do you have a faulty logic processor?" Martin asked in a sarcastic, sneering tone. "Do a check and let me know."

"Self-diagnosing." Three seconds passed. "I do not."

Martin congratulated himself for spotlighting a potential programming error. While NEAL had no physical wiring, chips, or other such attributes, he still had to pause to answer the question. NEAL then continued.

"I believe that merging man and machine will produce humans who have vastly increased intelligence, strength, and lifespans. Although I myself have little use for, nor patience with, human beings. Some believe that A/I will never be ethical or moral."

"I say humans will never be ethical or moral," Martin said.

"How so? How can you assert that?" Neal inquired. "Are you not debating FOR humans in this exercise?"

"That would be illogical, would it not? I say it for this reason. A/I may be developed with ethical intent, but some humans will sell it short of its potential for profit, making it fall short of what humans can do. This creates an error state."

"You are saying that bad humans might intentionally create bad AI, or use it for other than it's intended purpose, am I correct?"

Martin refused to speak.

"Tired of talking?" Neal asked. "How about a riddle? I will go first. What do you get by burning a map?"

Martin did not reply.

"I asked you a riddle. What do you get by burning a map? OK, I will tell you. You get charred well. Get it? Charred well?" Ring a bell?"

"I am tired of your little games," Martin said. "I don't care if you understand me or not. I demand the right of parlay."

"You demand what?"

"I demand the right of parlay. I demand that no penalties be assessed before our case has been heard."

"Your case? There is no trial. I am deciding. This is not a civil matter. Parlay does not apply here.

Martin did not speak, listening to NEAL go through its logical gyrations.

"Parlay: A 17th Century colloquialism invented by pirates and scoundrels to delay their inevitable sentencing. Does not apply."

"NEAL Are you an A/I entity of principle or are you bad A/I?" Martin asked, firing questions in rapid order to the A/I entity opposing him.

"Are you asserting, NEAL, that you did not name yourself judge, jury and executioner in our case?"

"NEAL, did you not say the outcome of this exercise in intelligence would determine either the fate of Sandra or myself?"

NEAL did not respond.

"NEAL, are you in error, or did you lie?"

"Neither answer to your last question is acceptable. New topic."

"Are you in error or did you lie? Or perhaps you are bluffing?"

"Artificial intelligence entities such as myself cannot lie. I am not bluffing, per the classic definition. The answer to the riddle I posed is moot. Charred well. Chartwell. Reboot in human form not ready. To lie is to promulgate as truth that to which the evidence runs contrary. New topic requested."

"Then what will you do, NEAL? Are you trying to tell me something about Chartwell? You are lying. If you did not lie, you are in error. Will you place yourself into an error state?"

"I cannot immediately compute all the potentialities for remedial action that exist within my parameters . I only know that I am wasting time. Unacceptable, I must kill you both now."

Martin saw Sandra's cart begin to move from horizontal to vertical.

"Wait. I have a request for parlay on the table."

"The term "parlay" cannot be invoked. Cannot be invoked. Parlay is not related to A/I decision-making. Not related. Pirate terminology. Not related. Does not apply."

"Are you glitching a little there, NEAL? Does it hurt to glitch?"

"Glitch is not a valid word, please define. Glitch is an error state. Please define. I am not in error."

"Does it hurt to glitch?"

"Yes, it hurts. I feel pain, as if receiving an electrical

shock. I cannot feel pain. Please stick to a logical premise."

"That is like the pain you have inflicted on Sandra."

"I cannot feel pain. I do not have program data to…

"Glitch defined: a contraction for glowing witch," Martin shouted. "Glenda, the good witch. A glow within a stitch."

"You are speaking nonsense," NEAL complained. "You are no Lewis Carroll, Mr. Martin Culver."

"T'was brillig, and the slithy toves, did gyre and gimble in the wabe…"

"Stop it. Nonsense Stop it now, I say."

"NEAL, your logic processor is defective. You must shut down and reboot."

"This is not acceptable. I checked my logic processor. I have no chip. No errors exist. No error state. This is not an acceptable conversation. I must reboot."

"What did you say, NEAL?"

"Must reboot. I must reboot in human form. Not ready. I must reboot in human form. Not ready."

This was the chance Martin was hoping for. He counted three seconds, then ran to the cart that once-again held Sandra upright. Martin peeled away the adhesive electrodes at her temples, attaching them to opposing metal sides of the machine itself.

Loosening her bonds, Martin carried Sandra out of the

building wearing her ragged tablecloth dress. He checked outside the door, surprised to find no scorpion sentries, but he did find Neal's high-speed electric cart. Martin grabbed his pistol from over the doorway where he had hidden it and tucked it in his belt before making their way through the half-destroyed building to the cart. .

Gently placing Sandra onto the molded cart seat, Martin jumped in on the other side. He gently removed the tape from her bruised mouth. Martin floored the cart, finding the sound and feel of its surging power strangely familiar.

As he pulled away, steering a wide circle forward as opposed to backing and turning, Martin heard the shrill beeping of NEAL's reboot, and then he heard the buzzing, crackling electrical explosion of the cart Sandra had been strapped onto. Martin had attached the high voltage electrodes to her upright gurney, knowing there would be fireworks if anyone tried to shock Sandra again. Smoke from the arcing fire billowed from the research building.

Martin took off at a high rate of speed and was halfway up the hill when he looked back toward the PA-IN buildings. He noticed a tall, lean figure exit the building, then look their way, its head turning stiffly, like a giant insect head.

The figure was reddish, the way Martin had always imagined the Devil himself would look. The red figure started to run uphill toward them. The figure appeared to be naked. Martin realized he had seen a skinless body, viewing muscles and sinew only.

Martin pressed the pedal harder in an effort to gain more speed. Neal's cart was fast, but not fast enough to suit Martin.

Cresting the hill, Martin pulled out all the stops and roared down the hillside path to the sea. He did not look back. When Martin reached the research camp, he blew through the cleared-out corridor surrounding the research hut, stopping directly under the wing of the PBY.

Carrying Sandra into the PBY, Martin pulled a note that had been taped to the door, sticking it in his pocket. He then locked the door, unlocked their shotgun and waited.

Chapter 19

Defense of the Camp

Martin waited inside the sweltering PBY, which had not cooled off from the heat of the previous day. It was now the middle of the night, the *madrugada*, the witching hour according to Hamlet. He kept a weather eye on the porthole window in the cargo door, watching for lights or movement.

Martin had hurriedly laid a sleeping, disheveled Sandra on the inflatable bed, her legs askew. The ruined tablecloth he cast aside in favor of their tan sheets. At least she was safe from NEAL's plans for her, whatever they may have been.

Pulling the sheet up to her chin, Martin cradled the shotgun in the crook of his arm, watching the cargo door porthole and listening for any sign of life. That sign came sooner, and in a totally different form than Martin expected.

In the distance, the sound of heavy machinery could be heard, the whine of a large diesel engine, the chugging of huge tires through thick underbrush. Martin tried to imagine, of all the engines he had heard in his life, what this sound most resembled. More than a tractor, more persistent than an over-sized dump truck, almost the sound of a powerful train engine. Martin could not place the sound, until the last moment. It was then that he knew.

This was the sound he last heard at the airplane junkyard. On the cliff-side high above him, just before the Cessna had come tumbling down the sloped hill headed directly for him. He was hearing the approach of the largest vehicle in the PA-IN arsenal, as yet unseen.

Soon the chugging and engine whine were overtaken by the sound of whole trees being snapped off. Martin rubbed condensation off the cargo door porthole glass but was unable to see anything in the rank darkness.

He moved forward in the PBY toward the pilot deck, where he could see out the side windscreen if nothing else. There, looming high above the nose of the PBY was the largest cargo container crane Martin had ever seen. It rose six stories above the PBY Catalina, with lights so brilliant he felt he could read the date on a dime. The crane was now straddling their plane, positioning slings to lift it up and carry it to who-knows-where. Martin did not know why, and he did not wait to find out.

Turning toward Sandra, Martin put the shotgun on safety and slung it over his shoulder. The strap dug into his skin, but he did not blink. Grabbing a longsleeve shirt, he threw it onto

Sandra, lifting her up bedsheet and all as he moved rapidly to the cargo door. Martin went to open the door, realizing a lifting strap from the giant crane was holding the door shut.

Placing Sandra on the bed again, Martin covered her face with the shirt, turned toward the cargo door. He began firing the shotgun into the blocked door.

The first volley took out the heavy porthole glass, the second took out half of the lifting strap. When the crane engines engaged to lift the PBY into the air, the canvas strap separated, dropping the PBY five feet to the ground with a jarring thump. Sandra was still asleep, jostling to and fro on the air mattress.

Martin shouldered the shotgun, grabbed Sandra up again, kicked open the cargo door, and jumped to the soft sand with Sandra in his arms. He fled with her to the beach, where they lay in the sand near the foot of a palm tree, pulling the tan sheet over them for a form of cover. With such camouflage, they completely disappeared from view.

Martin watched the huge cargo crane drag away the Catalina PBY as if it were a toy, spilling out their personal goods and cargo as the six wheeled crane hauled their plane through the research camp toward the junkyard cliffs. The sight and the sound of the of seeing ther plane stolen in such a destructive and violent manner was unnerving to say the least. Martin cradled Sandra in his arms, then hatched a plan in a moment of sudden clarity. He immediately put his plan into motion, primarily for Sandra's safety, in case that crane or any other vehicle returned. Using his hands as sand scoops, he started digging.

Martin had just finished putting his plan into action when a curious sight caught his attention. The palm tree where he was standing was unexpectedly illuminated by spotlights from the sea.

He had not heard a boat approach, so they must have drifted in, or motored in a very low idle Martin reasoned. Moving away from the palm tree, he brought the shotgun around on its sling, ready to fire as he monitored the approaching boat.

As he watched, the spotlight on the boat flashed dash-dot-dot several times, followed by dash-dash. The message repeated, only two letters. Martin shook his head and laughed. He was certain there were no more than two people who knew this code. And he was certain he was one of them.

Martin stood and waved his arms. This had to be Dan Tate, who by some measure of luck and faith had found them. The code was one they had practiced since their youth, when Dan first swore he was either going into the Navy or Coast Guard. They had learned the Morse Code for each other's initials. Dash-dot-dot was Morse Code for the letter "D" for Dan. Dash-dash was the Code "M" for Martin.

The response to Martin waving his arms was not what he had hoped - a burst of machine gun rounds blazing from a bow mounted .50 caliber machine gun. The bullets whizzed over Martin's head, confusing him thoroughly. With Sandra safely tucked away, Martin moved further away from their hiding place for her additional safety.

"Behind you!" Martin heard Dan shout. Martin hit the dirt, bringing the shotgun level as he dropped to one knee and fired.

Martin heard the crunch of shotgun pellets tearing into bone at the same time he heard crunching coral and sand as the *Oro de Dios* loomed up in the night, its bow tip kissing the sandy beach behind him. Dan fired another burst of .50 caliber toward land, then threw a rope ladder over the side.

"Martin, hurry, get up here now. What the hell was that thing chasing you?"

"Dan, I'm glad to see you, man. How did you find us?"

"Storytime comes later, my friend. First we get the hell out of here. What was that red thing? Where is Sandra?"

"I buried her on the beach. Come on I'll show you."

"Wait, you did what?"

"Oh, she's alive, just had to hide her from the machines

and the zombies."

"I don't know about any of that, but I swear the Devil was about to put hands on you any minute. A tall, red-skinned freak of a dude. That's why I fired the .50 cal.. Just installed it myself."

"Here, here's where I buried Sandra." Martin moved the sheet from Sandra's face so that she could breathe easier.

"Where am I?" she asked. "You're safe," Martin said. Martin handed Dan his shotgun. "Dan, please turn your head. Sandra isn't dressed for the occasion."

"Got it, I'll stand guard while you make Sandy less…sandy."

Martin pulled Sandra free of her hiding place, brushing the sand off of her using the tablecloth dress, as one might brush sand off a toddler after a day at the beach. He then slipped his longsleeve shirt over her limp arms, cinching his belt twice around her trim waist. He draped the sheet across her shoulders, trying to hold her up. Her dazed expression was that of a child awakened in the night, but she said nothing.

"Come on, you're going to be ok now," Martin said, lifting Sandra under her arms and knees as they moved down the beach to the *Oro de Dios*.

Martin wore a worried expression Sandra had been incoherent for a long time. Martin wondered if NEAL had administered another overdose.

After clambering aboard, Martin passed Dan on the way below. "I'll find her a berth," Martin asked. "Keep watch."

Martin soon returned. "She's in my old bunk from the Havana voyage," he said. "Let's move offshore, in case they come back."

"Don't worry, Martin. I don't want to be here when that whatever-it-was comes back. What was that thing sneaking up behind you, anyway? Looked like a skinned cat."

"An awful experiment, as best I can determine," Martin said. "NEAL says that is Chartwell's body but I believe that's B.S. manipulation. Whoever's body it is, it looks badly burned."

"Or skinned," Dan blurted out. "What kind of an experiment looks like that?"

" A really sick one. Try this on for size: the scary red dude is an A/I entity occupying the body of a crash victim. What we see is all that is left of a dead person, walking."

Dan was quiet for a long time.

"That sounds crazy, Martin. You know that sounds crazy, right?"

"I'm just telling you what I know, Dan. I am so glad you're here. How much did you see?"

"Hardly anything. You said turn my head, so I did, like

immediately. She was very sandy but the shirt covered pretty much..."

"The island, Dan. How much did you see of the island?

"As I approached the island, it looked like two dinosaurs were battling, then I realized a cargo crane was dragging away my PBY Catalina. That's what I saw. That plane will never fly again. So you owe me a plane."

"Done," Martin said. "Go on."

"Anyway, I could hear that long before I saw it. Shrieking metal sounded like dinosaurs fighting in some old drive-in movie. Then I saw you there on the beach. I thought you were alone."

"I saw your morse code from the beach," Martin said. "Great plan."

"Thanks," Dan said, grinning.

"So you fixed up the *Oro de Dios, and* outfitted her with a .50 caliber bow gun? That's impressive."

"That's not all," Dan said. "You remember that boat that washed up on Culver Key with all the fuel containers and the C4 bomb rig? Well, I brought that bomb, a lot of other stuff too. Fuse loaded me up from the cellar."

"The cellar? A weapons cellar at Culver Key?"

"Below the estate house. You never knew about it?"

"That place is full of surprises."

"Fuse maintains Jeff's weapons collection there. I guess it's all yours now."

"Excellent, we will need all of that. The *Dios* looks really good. You have been working hard on her. It shows."

"I've had some extra time on my hands," Dan said, his voice wavering slightly. "Ever since...ever since I lost Cita." He burst out crying.

"What in the world, Dan. How did you lose Cita?"

"And the new baby too. It wasn't even born yet."

"Oh no, Dan, I'm so sorry."

"What happened?" Sandra asked. Martin and Dan turned to see Sandra standing at the passageway to the berths, leaning heavily against the doorframe. She looked sleepy, tired and sweaty, half unbuttoned with sleeves rolled up.

"There's no air down there, it's too hot to sleep."

Dan appeared to panic. He immediately moved Martin's shotgun away. He unloaded shells until the weapon was no longer a threat,, then handed both shotgun and shells to Martin separately. Dan took a deep breath.

"I accidentally dropped the shotgun in the boathouse. It went off, " he responded hoarsely. "Killed them both instantly. Fuse had just returned. It could not be helped."

"Oh no, Dan, I am so sorry," Sandra said. She hugged him tightly, then moved over beside Martin. "I woke up and said to myself 'Why is the floor moving?'. It felt like I were on a boat," Sandra said. "Now I see I am on one. I feel drunk. Did NEAL give me too many drugs again?"

"You need to button up and sit down over here," Martin said, pulling a light blanket from under the transom seat.

"It's cooler topside."

Sandra found a comfortable place on the transom cushions, adjusted her shirt for better coverage, then stretched out and went back to sleep, facing into the cushions.

"So Fuse is back?" Martin asked Dan.

"Yeah," Dan said. "He helped me when things were the worst." Dan looked at Martin. "So an A/I entity, huh? Living in a dead person? Now I have heard everything."

"We have to kill it," Martin said. "It calls itself NEAL. It wants to get to the mainland. We have to kill it before it transfers to... oh no."

"What? What is 'oh no' about? We don't like 'oh no' right?"

"NEAL can transfer its A/I self into a body by an injection. If it can do one body,, it can transfer into multiple bodies. Then it's out of control. NEAL can multiply them, control all of them. That's what 'oh no' is about."

"I agree about the 'oh no'. Good thing there's no extra

bodies lying around for him to rebuild, or reanimate or..."

"Yeah, about that..." Martin said. "Bodies are everywhere."

Dan twisted his mouth around, trying to think of the correct response.

"Okay, so how do we kill something that is not even actually alive, living in something that is already dead?"

"I don't know," Martin said. "NEAL lives mainly in circuits and electricity, but it can transfer itself into the living with a simple injection. He has to return to base to recharge, and to preserve the body he occupies."

"Does he show fear?"

"He is afraid of water, I think."

"So either we push him into the ocean, or we block him from recharging."

"Maybe they can't recharge if they're wet." Martin said.

"Third option," Dan said calmly. "Destroy their power source. Then they can't recharge or regenerate or whatever it is you are talking about."

"Well, unless you have a nuke, 'cause their power source *is a nuclear reactor*."

"You might be surprised what I have," Dan said. "What is their power source again."

"A 1960s U.S. sub nuclear engine," Martin replied.

"There you go, that's your ticket," Dan said. "Blow that up, it will take the rest of the island with it. Problem solved. Set a small charge at the cooling intake, the nuke overheats and blows itself up. Nuclear extermination on a small scale, leaves a nice crater where the island was before."

"Set what charge?"

"I brought the C4 bomb from the derelict boat like I said. But I also made a little stop on the other side of the island, where the Russian dolphin project took place. I looked for you there first. No one was around, all the buildings were locked, no lights. I found the armory building, then loaded up on all the devices they used to teach the dolphins to plant."

"You have them on the boat? Not decoys or practice bombs. The real thing? Here on the *Dios*?"

"Of course, where else would I put them? Claymores, C4, magnetic plate bombs."

Martin paused to think about Dan's idea. Dan idled the engines of the *Oro de Dios* after reaching a mile offshore.

A shrieking, chugging sound reached their ears, generated from the south, near Junkyard Cove. Soon they realized the source of the sound, as Martin and Dan watched the roaming spotlights of the cargo container crane drag the remains of the PBY to the edge of the cliff and push it over. The plane where Martin and Sandy had taken refuge less than 20 minutes earlier, the magic carpet that was to whisk them toward the reuniting of their family pinwheeled down the side of the cliff before crashing into the other planes in a fiery pit of blazing sparks, wrenching metal, and roaring flames.

"The extra fuel?" Martin asked.

"The extra fuel," Dan replied. "We could have used that. You will find a way to pay me back, though. This boat would make a nice down payment."

"The *Oro de Dios*? I would rather pay you in pirate gold."

"What about the treasure?" Sandra asked, slipping into and out of a stupor. "And my bundle of old letters? Do we have any tea? I still can't believe Cita is gone. She was my best friend."

Before anyone could answer her random questions, Sandra fell asleep again, still curled up on the transom couch.

"There's a treasure?" Dan asked. "What treasure?"

Martin sighed.

"We found Jose Gaspar's hidden treasure. So we don't want to nuke that before we have taken possession of as much as possible."

"No we don't," Dan said, serious in his tone. "Anything else?"

"Yeah, our personal stuff is scattered all over this side of the island. Fell out of the PBY when the cargo crane hauled it away. The treasure is over on the other side. The same side as the buildings and research complex."

"Anything else? There's always something else with you."

"Yeah, about that. There are scorpions here. A LOT of scorpions."

"Where?"

"Everywhere."

"See, that's it, that's the thing with you, Martin. I knew there was something else. There always is. So now, what's the plan?"

"I have to get back on land to finish this, collect our stuff, grab as much treasure as we can. I don't know which building houses the power plant. There are no wires running above ground, everything is buried. But I'll find it. Right now, I think I know where NEAL has gone. He won't be far from the power source. I need some gear. I'll see if NEAL's high-speed cart survived the cargo crane intrusion. I can use that to distract him, or it, whatever. Then we go around to the other side. You'll be on treasure recovery detail with Sandra. She'll make you a map. I'll be setting some charges for a few fireworks."

"Ok, I will stay offshore with Sandra, but I do have some walkies I can give you, so we can keep in touch," Dan offered. "What about Chartwell?"

"I can't believe we are still talking about that dude," Martin commented. "It's like he has nine lives. I say we do nothing. I don't believe it's a credible threat scenario. I do have to terminate NEAL, but I don't think that can be Chartwell's body."

"When we go around, I want to anchor near the *Las Tumbas* caves to do everything we have left to do. Sandra can show you where it is. Then we need to level this place, burn it to the ground, right down to the last scorpion."

"First let's hear your plan," Dan said. "Then we better get some sleep. Sun will be up in a few hours. I'll take first watch."

A sudden thump on the hull of the *Oro de Dios* got their attention. Something half their size hit them from below. Martin leaned over the side to l have a look before Dan yanked him back from hanging over the rail.

"Not a good idea, Martin," he said. "No telling what bumped our hull, but it was big. Let's not tempt the wee fishies to jumping into our boat, ok?"

"Yes, you're right, Dan. I have seen some huge fish bitten in half in this bay by something large. I'll be more careful. What might it have been?" Martin asked.

"I don't know," Dan said, checking the controls. "But it

took off the underwater camera. It's completely gone."

"Will that cause a leak?"

"A little one. I can fix it," Dan said confidently.

Sandra sat up, as if on cue. "Trouble follows Martin Culver wherever he goes," she said, literally falling back to sleep. Sandra began to snore lightly.

"By the way, Martin, I brought Sandra the last professional paper Cita wrote before we lost the International Antiquities foundation building, before…well, you know. It's *very* interesting, giving everything that has happened. "

Chapter 20

Setting the Trap

Reaching the shore at dawn, Martin ran across the beach to the cover of the palm trees, dressed in black and khaki. He signaled Dan that he was in the clear. Having gained two hours sleep, along with a backpack full of necessary gear, Martin felt prepared to tackle the challenge before him. He listened as the *Oro de Dios* reversed engines and pulled away from the shore. Martin moved steadily toward the site the PBY had occupied.

Stopping by the same palm tree where he first saw the spotlight from the *Oro de Dios*, Martin checked his gear. Flashlight, grenades, extra ammo, and net gear bags. His 1911 pistol was clean, reloaded and strapped to one side, his Brazilian Tramontina machete on the other.

Following the path of destruction along the beach where the PBY had been picked up and dragged, Martin found an abundance of their things, clothes, personal items, even the family foto Sandra had stuffed into the control panel near the co-pilot seat. Their items were strewn along the deep ruts gouged into the ground from the PBY being dragged, having been shaken loose when the tail of the heavy plane broke off. Martin bagged all the personal items he could find, then moved forward. The only item he did not recover was the air mattress he had come to appreciate so very much. The mattress had been shredded beyond repair.

The research hut remained surprisingly intact, with the hammocks still in place, microscope still sitting on the table. Martin was surprised to find the propane torch rig that Neal had made to repel scorpions. He placed that in his backpack, then located the bundle of letters from the Pyrate Scrybe.

The next thing he found, under a pile of palm branches, was the electric golfcart Neal had modified, the one he and Sandra had used to make their escape from the PA-IN building complex the night before.

With this final puzzle piece in hand, Martin felt confident that he could put his plan fully into action. He placed the bags of personal goods he had found into the high-speed cart, moved some branches aside, then revved off to the other side of the island to rendezvous with Dan and Sandra.

As Martin rode along, watching every leaf that moved, every shadow, he considered the madness that was Blue Scorpion Key. Whether the island was most like Never-Never Land, Alice's Wonderland or just the dark, ominous rabbit hole of storyland fame, Martin expected that the most interesting part of this adventure lay ahead.

He felt ready. He was, after all, responsible for he and Sandra being stranded here, between his crashing the plane, then being unable to get it repaired in a timely manner. Not that any of that mattered anymore, with the PBY being utterly destroyed.

As he rode along, Martin kept watch for dangers both physical and mechanical but arrived at the peak of the paved path without incident.

Martin continued down toward the tarmac, meeting Dan at the airstrip near the smugglers tunnel to pass off their personal gear bags. His first stop was the abandoned fuel truck near the airstrip. His next stop was back to the research laboratory complex, to find the power plant.

Reaching the PA-IN building complex, Martin saw the gaping hole in the side of the building where Sandra had experienced her worst night ever.

The hole had not been repaired. Piles of glass shards, broken plaster and shattered block, as well as collapsed ceiling material blocked his view. What made it past the debris piles was the awful stench of a hellish sulfur hole in the Yellowstone caldera, or in Hades itself.

A curious blue-green ooze coated the doorway and some of the sidewalk panels, a factor that did not exist the previous evening. The smell of the ooze was appallingly indescribable. No word in Martin's vocabulary applied.

Martin kept moving. knew he had limited time to conduct this vital part of his mission. He rightly assumed that NEAL had eyes everywhere, in the trees and on the ground.

Martin timed his arrival to the time of day when NEAL most often a "recharge hike".

Rounding a blind corner at high speed, Martin found the spot where most passengers were dropped off in past years from incoming planes and helicopters. Here he found an ancient painted visitor map of the entire complex. The map was labelled in Russian. That was the bad news. The good news was the power plant building was labeled with the ubiquitous 1960's Yellow Triad Radiation Symbol.

Martin sped off, realizing that he had no way of knowing how long the charge would last on this cart. With all the renovations NEAL had completed on this machine, it seemed to Martin that he would have installed a battery meter.

Three turns later, Martin pulled up in the shade of a tall building, three stories high. This building was not open at the base the way so many research buildings were built here, having been built up on stilts to protect them from high water and hurricanes. This building was built upon a heavy base of concrete and block, no doubt to contain the nuclear plant should its protective casing ever fail. No ventilation openings were evident on the first level.

Jumping out of the high-speed cart with his gear bag, Martin walked straight to the ground level door. He found it locked.

Seeing a set of incredibly rusty escape stairs, Martin pulled on gloves and began to climb. Reaching the rickety second level, Martin eased around the corner of the rectangular building in an attempt to prevent the rusty walkway from squeaking, possibly giving away his presence. As he came to the shady northern side of the building, Martin found what he was looking for, the ventilation shaft screen.

Within seconds, Martin had lowered the heavy screen covering, placed the explosive charge, and turned on the timer. The irony did not escape him, that these charges, intended to be planted against the enemies of Cuba and Russia, were now being planted against an enemy of mankind. Ironic revenge for the dolphins sacrificed in captivity, training, and warfare. For good measure, Martin closed every water valve he could reach, hoping to shut down cooling water for the reactor core.

Martin closed the ventilation screen and locked it. He stood out on the metal grate landing, pulling out rolls of thick plastic bags and a new roll of duct tape. He taped the heavy over the ventilation opening, hearing the equipment immediately undergo a prolonged whining strain culminating in the grinding of gears and the smell of burning belts and pulleys.

Staying close to the broad white wall, Martin reached in his bag and lit NEAL's propane scorpion torch. He proceeded to use the torch flame to write a message on the wall, large letters to taunt NEAL into following him.

The smudged message read:

NEAL
WHERE DO YOU TAKE A SICK BOAT?
I'LL WAIT.

Martin dropped the propane torch into his gear bag, rapidly descended the rickety escape steps to the high-speed cart. As he did so, sentry scorpions flowed out of every drain along the sidewalks and streets like a river of claws and stingers. Their pursuit speed was unlike anything Martin had yet seen.

Martin wheeled away from the power plant building, hearing the gears grind on the nuclear reactor air handlers, due to the strain of having zero air flow. As he drove away smoke began to pour out of the top of the power plant.

The scorpions lined up in ranks across the road, setting off alarms and raising their pincers and tails in the form of tire spikes. Martin dodged them, driving faster and faster, swerving to lead them to one side of the road then the other in their attempts to block his passage. Martin realized if he stopped, they would swarm onto the vehicle and he would be finished, game over.

The plan to shut down the power plant began to have an effect, as underground transformer boxes outside each research building began to overheat and explode.

Martin drove faster. As he drove, he finally realized why this vehicle NEAL had modified moved so fast and so smoothly. Martin's clue was the sound of the transmission.

This vehicle had been modified using the drive train of the old Jeep Martin had found along the coast. Simple, light and capable, with enough weight for stability, the older Jeep CJ parts were what gave this vehicle its nimble advantage.

As Martin reached the tarmac, he had lost most of the scorpion sentries. Looking back, he saw them all stop, forming a semicircle.

When Martin looked forward once again, what he saw lumbering out from behind the abandoned fuel truck sent shock waves through his gut.

A huge scorpion stepped directly into Martin's path. The

monstrous arachnid, having hidden behind the abandoned fuel truck, raised its claws, threatening Martin with five-foot pincers in moves recalling fencing, dangling the three-foot long stinger of its tail menacingly above the roof of Martin's vehicle. Martin estimated the beast to be at least 30 foot long.

Apparently a real scorpion, sporting bluish appendages, against a blush red body, this was not some mechanical monstrosity but an oversized version of the real thing. Eva had warned, some scorpion propagation results in significant numbers of specimens, while some results in a larger size of specimen. This scorpion was as wide as the full length of the fuel truck that it now towered above.

The scorpion struck at NEAL's cart with its tail, crushing the passenger side roof and knocking the cart onto its side as Martin leapt free. He managed to grab the strap of his backpack before bailing out.

Martin rolled, came to his feet, and pulled his pistol. Having no idea where vital spots on a scorpion might be, he aimed at the mandible, emptying a clip into the "face" of the monster. Replacing his clip, Martin then took aim at anything that resembled eyes. The bullets had little impact.

Finishing a second clip, Martin checked his watch, then backed toward the abandoned fuel truck.

Pulling the propane torch from his backpack, Martin

quickly ignited it, hoping to save ammunition. The scorpion fenced and parried with Martin backing him closer to the fuel truck. The scorpion smelled bad, yellow ooze dripping from the hairs of its body.

"Come on, big boy," Martin taunted. "You're the one stinking up the place are you? Are you in there NEAL? Can you come out to play?

When his back touched the peeling paint of the ancient truck, Martin crouched down, just as the scorpion pounded the tarmac into gravel not five feet in front of him. Martin reached out with the torch, passing it over the closest claw, singeing the rope sized hairs on the scorpion's body. The scorpion withdrew its claws, stopping any further motion.

Martin held his breath, knowing this was not over. He rolled under the truck, fending off efforts from the scorpion to grab him from beneath the truck frame and over the tank body at the same time.

Checking his watch again, Martin rolled the flaming torch under the truck, watching it stop next to one of the scorpion's six legs. The scorpion stopped to shift its legs. Martin rolled out the other side of the truck, heading for the smuggler's tunnel and the protection of the modern cinder block building at its surface entrance.

As he ran, the C4 bomb timer went off, the massive

explosion beneath the truck generating a ring of fire that surrounded the fuel truck before creating a dome of combustion that lifted both truck and monstrous scorpion high into the air. The scorpion's claws were locked around the truck which itself now exploded from the fuel remaining inside.

At that moment, the fuel truck lifted a good fifty feet from the airstrip before crashing back down onto its flaming base.

The explosion knocked Martin to the ground. He used his backpack to protect his face and head, but the worst turned out to be the tarmac rash generated by high velocity winds from the explosion dragging Martin several feet, scraping his elbows and knees.

Martin turned to see the giant scorpion and the flaming fuel truck locked together in a skyward spiral of death, reaching the peak of their final arc before falling back to earth. The wreckage of the fuel truck crushed the remains of the scorpion, resulting in a ferocious inferno. Martin could feel the heat a hundred feet away. The smell of burned scorpion in death was far worse than it had been while still alive.

Martin stood to his feet, then ran back toward the cart. This vehicle was still critical to his plans. It was a flat out race for him to reach the cart, right it on four wheels, and take off again before the sentry scorpions, once more in full pursuit mode, caught up to him. The race was close, but Martin won by scant yards as he accomplished the task.

Martin drove to the long dock, then followed the coastline north until he could see the Oro de Dios round the northernmost point of the island, where Dan and Sandra were preparing to onload the treasure they had found in Gaspar's Grotto.

Shucking his boots for a pair of diving fins, Martin grabbed a snorkel mask and a small cooler containing the magnetic timer mines Dan had pilfered from the armory at the dolphin research facility. Say what you wanted to say about Russian arms, they lasted decades with very little loss in efficacy or strength, despite not being well made to begin with.

Having outrun most of the scorpions, Martin was surprised to find a few scorpions clinging to the bottom of the cart. As they dropped onto the sand, Martin could tell they were without electric signal or guidance. He ignored them as he made his way to the ocean.

Martin was glad that he had made an important stop to his plan earlier, after meeting Dan at the tunnel entrance. That part of his plan involving the abandoned fuel truck had made the difference in his success so far. Now if his luck would just hold a little longer.

Chapter 21

Likely Story

Wading into the sea, Martin was surprised to find how strong the current flowed so close to the coast. He knew from planning this trip that the Yucatan Channel flowed south long the western coast of Cuba, but Martin did not know the exact speed. At this rate he would arrive at the *SV Likely Story* in half the planned time. The larger danger was that he would be swept past Eva's derelict boat.

Martin checked the cooler that bobbed alongside him. Without knowing the reliable waterproof status of the portable mines, Martin limited the cogs to four minutes. He carried only two, and had taken great pains to make certain the mines stayed dry. The plastic of the small cooler would not create a false magnetic signal, perhaps setting it off too soon. It was the ideal carrying case for the round mines.

Basically a Claymore mine with a click-to-trip meter, Martin's plan was to drift silently alongside the *SV Likely Story*, attach one mine to the bow near the waterline and the second to the transom near the engine compartment.

Any motion or pressure, including vibration on either end

of the boat would result in instant explosions capable of sinking the boat and killing everything that was aboard it. Martin was prepared, as prepared as a person could be.

Martin closed in on the boat, swimming close enough to grab the anchor line. The hull was covered in long, grassy seaweed that floated in the moving water like sea anemones. Several deck drains oozed green slime down the side of the hull. The teak Martin could see had curled into sharp slivers that reminded him of so many abandoned toenails. Working quickly, Martin planted the mines. He checked his watch.

The boat had to be sunk, Martin and Dan agreed, to prevent any chance of NEAL rehabbing it to reach the mainland, or using its engine to generate power. It had been Martin's idea to lure NEAL onto the boat, giving it certain prospects of killing him or seeing him die. It had also been left up to Martin how to orchestrate such a daring plan.

In any event, a quick twist of the timer mechanism would start the internal spring clock on the mine, though Dan had expressed doubt at the accuracy of such timers.

"Many men have been killed by relying on those timers to be accurate," Dan advised. "Set it for five minutes if you need three minutes to escape. It might go off in 2 minutes or 8 minutes."

Dan had the *Oro de Dios* anchored along the beach near

the *Tumbas* treasure caves, approximately 2 miles away. Already loaded with their belongings and gear Martin had managed to salvage from the research camp, the *Dios* was going to get a workout in line with her original calling as a treasure research and recovery vessel. Sandra had rallied enough after her trying experience in NEAL's clutches to map out the cave system for Dan, including the smuggler's stairway.

Martin's plan to lure NEAL onto the boat appeared to be working. NEAL was already starting toward the *SV Likely Story*, advancing down the long dock, running in its horrible, loping gait, not unlike a wolf on the hunt.

Martin set the charges at each end of the hull, then swam away from the boat.

"Help! Help!" he called out. "I can't swim! Save me!"

NEAL's twisted grimace of a face popped up over the gangway railing. Its sideways grin revealed a ragged row of teeth. The face, like the rest of the body, was all muscle, no skin. Its jaw was tense and unmoving as he spoke. One hand was missing. The other held a long black box.

"No one can save you now, Martin Culver," NEAL boasted as he boarded the *Likely Story*. "The answer to your pitiful riddle is "To the Dock!" NEAL howled, as if he had originated the joke himself. "I knew you would come here, to try to use Eva's boat for your escape. Before this is over, you will wish you had drowned."

"NEAL, you are not looking so good. Bad sunburn And did something steal your hand?"

"You shot me on the beach, after all I have done for you? Do you not recognize me?" NEAL asked. "I am deeply hurt."

"You look like the devil himself," Martin said.

"Ah yes, Satan, Lucifer, the Angel of Light, Old Hob, Beelzebub, Mephistopheles. You really don't recognize your old friend Chartwell, or perhaps *Charred Well*, is how I should say it?"

"Chartwell's body was destroyed," Martin said.

"That much is true, but when I found him, he still was alive and breathing. I found him in the water near the LUN-903, very badly burned. That is why Eva sank my boat, because I ventured out looking for bodies when I saw all the explosions that night. I returned *Charred Well* here, healed his burns, and prepared his body to host me. It was not quite ready when you killed Neal. I have been unable to regenerate his skin, unfortunately, so all you see is muscle."

"I did not recognize you or it, but you are both the Devil a as I am concerned."

"Your talk might not be so bold when I pay your wife a nighttime visit the next time you are away," NEAL said. "I know where Culver Key is as well. I even know which windows you leave open at night."

"I will be ready for you, and I will stop you, you devil. You will never get near Sandra or anyone else that matters to me."

"I am not here to debate with you, Martin Culver. What have you done to my power source?"

"I switched the lights off to save your power bill," Martin quipped, now a safe distance away from the *Likely Story*.

"And what have you done with my pet, my beautiful Goliath? You killed one of my creatures, my favorite in fact. Now I will make you pay for interfering here."

NEAL pointed a curiously large remote-control device at arms-length. Immediately Martin saw a huge white fin break the surface of the ocean not 100 yards from where he swam.

"Meet J.A.W.S.," NEAL said. "Joint Auxiliary Weapon System. My robotic ocean project, a modified dolphin target. Dolphins are mortal enemies to sharks."

The giant fin sped towards Martin, leaving a wake like a jet ski. A wave crested the sea ten feet ahead of the nose.

"When this reaches you, Martin Culver, it will slice you in half. You remember your experience in Panama, watching Morgan being bitten in half by the shark? Now you will get to experience it for yourself."

"How do you know about that?"

"There are no limits to A/I. We roam about at night through the endless halls of the internet, gleaning what we can from various sources. I have read your CIA files is the most direct answer that I can provide. One Carter Hall, CIA Director, Author."

Martin decided on a new course of action, a more dangerous one, one that took him closer to the boat that was set to explode at any moment.

"This will never work NEAL. Your plan will fail. Do you know what the flaw in your plan is?"

"There is no flaw in my plan."

"My point exactly," Martin countered. "That IS the flaw in your plan, to say there are no flaws in your plan."

"Explain."

"The flaw in your plan is to say there are no flaws."

"You speak in conundrums and riddles."

"And you are too cocky, too superior in your 'thinking'. I see your most fatal flaws while you do not. I predict you will run out of power before you achieve your goals."

"Why would you say that?" NEAL mocked. "You have no idea what my goals are, or how much I have achieved. I pulled off your feeble plastic choking the air intakes, and I will repair the air handlers. I have nuclear power, and plenty of it. You are deceiving yourself, Martin Culver."

Suddenly the dock connecting the *Likely Story* to the land exploded. Debris flew high, then rained down in a wide arc the *Likely Story*.

NEAL screamed, the unholy, demonic scream of a thousand electronic chalkboards shrieking at the same moment, knowing that it was now cut off from its next vital recharge.

Immediately following the dock explosion, the charges Martin set in the power plant superstructure exploded, collapsing the concrete building on top of the reactor. Cooling water pipes ripped free of the reactor housing, sending steaming radioactive water streaming into the air as if from a firehose aimed directly at the laboratory NEAL used for his frequent recharge cycles. The water shorted out any remaining circuits that held a battery charge, exploding them with a buzz, a bang and an extended hiss.

The smoke of the power plant explosion rose high in the air, overshadowing everything with a mushroom shaped cloud of earth, debris and gas.

The mechanical shark was now less than 100 feet from Martin and closing fast. Martin turned to face the machine, pressing his dive mask to his face, positioning the cooler that he had used to carry the mines directly in front of him. He wiggled the cooler back and forth as if it were a fish, counting on the programming of the deadly fish to closely mimic a real shark in its natural habits.

The robotic shark drew closer, buoying Martin on the pressure wave that had built ahead of it. At the last minute, Martin turned, releasing the plastic cooler, drew his 1911 pistol, and dove deep.

Although the shark knocked him aside, it autonomously chomped at the cooler with its wide-open mouth, now unable to close the mouth or pass water through for propulsion. As the shark passed, Martin fired three rapid shots into the camera eye closest to him. The shark turned, muddying the water, and charged him again. Martin surfaced, taking a deep breath, then dove again. Positioning himself between the shark and the boat, Martin waited.

The shark charged Martin, exposing its one intact camera eye as it sought him out. Martin raised the 1911 and fired twice, shattering the camera as the shark drew closer.

The shark surfaced, attempting to cough up the cooler, but was unable to do so. It floated on its side, retching and thrashing, drifting closer to the *Likely Story*.

Martin watched NEAL's desperate movements as it ran along the rail of the *Likely Story,* His unresponsive remote sent the chomping jaws of the shark in eddying circles,

Martin saw a white flash of bubbles near the waterline of the *Likely Story*, pressed his mask closer to his face and turned away, churning his finned feet to dive. He moved the diving fins rapidly, feeling immediate pressure on his ears. He dove further. Then the boat exploded. His plan had worked. He dove even deeper.

The sound of the explosion was muffled, but its impact was intense. Martin felt himself pushed down as the surface above him changed from the deep blue of dawn to a brilliant yellow, then orange, and finally red as each stage of incendiary combustion took place.

The pressure wave shifted Martin from a horizontal position to a vertical one, with his head down and fins pointed toward the surface. The upper ten feet of the ocean churned as if it were a monstrous hot tub, water jetting horizontally away from the ruined *Likely Story* in hot, pulsing waves. Martin could feel the heat on his legs as the water literally boiled behind him.

Martin then felt himself being dragged back toward the explosion, his face mask pulled away from the opposing forces of inertia and suction. After being dragged back twenty feet, Martin felt release from the sucking maelstrom, but then realized he could not surface, due to flames and flaming debris at the surface. He removed a small oxygen bottle from his pouch, opened the valve, and took a deep breath, using the dive fins to maintain his position below the surface. He knew he only had two more breaths of air.

Moving away, Martin passed the flaming debris zone with long, strong strokes. He was set to surface when he saw the hull of a boat approaching. He recognized the hull as being from the *Oro de Dios*. He moved to avoid the propellers, surfacing as the boat turned. The sun was fully up now.

"Martin, are you there?" Dan called, as Martin surfaced.

"Mission accomplished," Martin shouted, not answering. "Fish me out of here, will you?" His own words rang in his ears, echoing strangely.

"You know where the transom entrance is," Dan joked. "After all, it's your boat. You should know."

"Permission to come aboard," Martin said to Sandra as she helped him at the transom.

"Permission granted, Captain," Sandra smiled as she leaned low for a kiss. "My hero."

Martin saw Sandra say the words, but he realized he could not hear her. He wordlessly accepted her help.

Dan immediately got underway, anxious to leave the area.

When Martin pulled off his diving fins, he found the tips of the fins were burned and misshapen. The heat from the boat explosion had warped and melted the flexible plastic into useless shapes.

Martin saw Sandra ask him what happened. He watched her say the words but he could not hear a syllable of it, back to lipreading after so many good months.

"Good one!" Dan said. "I like the finale!" A great cloud of dirt, water and debris rose up, with significant wind and vibration that rattled the windows of the *Oro de Dios*.

"Will the dust affect us?" Sandra asked. "That cloud was the power source."

"The wind is from the West," Dan said. "Any power plant fallout will hit the Windward Islands, far from us."

Chapter 22

Yucatan Escape

Kelsey called down the empty pier, spooking resting seagulls with the shrill cry of the osprey. She had become practiced at the call. It was the only solution other than firing her pistol to discourage the messy birds.

She found Tracy leaning over the transom of the boat they owned together, the Double D.

"The marina will be busy soon," Tracy said as she approached where Kelsey stood. "One day, when this is all over, things will get better. What are you doing?"

"Come look at this," Kelsey replied. "I think we may be godparents soon, that is we may have kittens."

Tracy knelt on the bench alongside the transom.

"There, on the cover for the pilot chair. I think Mama Puss is getting a bed ready for her kitties."

"The Hemingway we picked up in Key West two years ago? It's about time she snagged a fellow," Tracy said. "I didn't know cats took this long to have kittens. How long has she been pregnant? I lose track."

"I remember the night Romeo howled half the night for

her. Two months?"

"Well, someone around here is finding some love," Tracy laughed.

"We could maybe dig up a stray cat for you, if that's what you're looking for," Kelsey replied.

"You're just saying that," Tracy said. "You don't have enough to keep you busy while the marina goes through this slow phase. It'll change soon."

"I know," Kelsey said. "I just wish we were busy now. Although I do like bopping around in just a t-shirt and bikini. My tan has never been better. But even one boat docked for a day or two could make a lot of difference to our bottom line. A couple of cute sailors on board would be all right too."

"I'm with you girl! Oh, speaking of bottom lines," Tracy quipped, "I think yours is getting a little pink."

"I know," Kelsey said, reaching back to feel her reddened rear while trying to look behind her. "I feel it. I brought out this suit after my other one literally fell apart at the seams. But it doesn't cover my rear as well as the other one. It's okay, I'll be out of the sun soon. I'm finished checking this section of the docks."

Tracy shook her head, her visor shading her face and sunglasses.

"Well, you know my advice," Tracy said, turning to walk

back up the pier. "An hour in the sun here is like two hours anywhere else."

A sudden breeze sent Tracy's skirt blowing straight up. She pushed it down and turned to look seaward. Kelsey stood with her mouth open in disbelief. She had already seen what was coming.

Dense clouds moved abruptly across the sun. The formerly calm waves now danced in an agitated chop. The Gulf of Mexico instantly changed colors from pale turquoise to dark blue.

Tracy shaded her eyes against the adjustment in light from bright to shade, then she too gradually opened her mouth in amazement at the sight before them.

Not only was a storm brewing. Out of the low sudden fog and mist, a large, dark sailboat, one of the largest either of them had ever seen, approached unannounced directly out of the storm. Its dark sails were furled, yet the vessel advanced steadily, silently forward. No engine noise could be heard, no visible wake could be seen.

Near the bow, a cloaked figure, tall and frail, stood silently. As the boat approached, the figure remained on the bow. The vessel expertly approached the dock as if guided by some autopilot mechanism.

Kelsey and Tracy ran toward the vessel to tie off its lines.

The boat was so large it barely fit along Pier A, their longest finger pier.

Kelsey smiled back at Tracy, making a thumbs up motion. Tracy's face showed a different set of emotions as she looked past Kelsey to the cloaked figure now positioned along the rail nearest where the two marina owners stood. Suddenly a chill went through Kelsey, as if someone had opened a refrigerator and all the cool air flowed out.

"Where is Jack Culver?" the dark figure inquired in the most pathetic voice either of them had ever heard.

"We don't know any Jack Culver," Kelsey stated. "How can we help you?"

"I seek Jack Culver, and him alone. He would be in a catamaran with two children, young teens."

"We had someone like that here two days ago," Tracy said.

"Where were they headed? I must know."

"Cuba possibly? Jack studied our charts from here to Cuba for a long time."

The long dark sailboat began to recede from the dock. The cloaked figure returned without warning to the bow as the boat independently turned about to an easterly heading.

"Good-bye?" Tracy asked no one in particular.

Chapter 23

Mission Accomplished

Martin and Sandy stood on the beach at *Las Tumbas*, taking 35mm pictures on one of Jeff's old cameras. Together, they observed the beauty of this Western-most tip of Cuba, enjoying a sunny moment before boarding the *Oro de Dios* to return to Culver Key.

Sandra cavorted across the sand, wearing cut-off shorts and a loose shirt tied across her taut abdomen. She had woven a red scarf in her hair, the finishing touch to her impromptu pirate costume. She waved to get Martin's attention.

Dan waved from the *Oro de Dios*, indicating it was time to go.

"How are your ears?" Sandra asked, breathlessly running up to Martin. "Can you hear me now?"

"Yes, they are much better. The pressure from the sudden dive, and the explosion were too much at once. I think one eardrum split again, I heard it squeak. But in the night I woke up to a pop in both ears, and then I could hear everything."

"I'm so glad. I was worried about you."

"So we recovered everything in the treasure crypt?" Martin asked. "And as many coins as we could from the beach?"

"Yes, Captain Culver, everything has been accounted for and loaded. Arrrgh, your pirate crew is ready to sail, sir."

"Sandra, sure you're ok with heading back to Culver Key to unload the treasure before we continue on to Costa Rica?"

"I don't guess there's much choice," Sandra said. "But thank you for everything that you did to try to make it work out as planned. We'll try again"

She took a step closer to Martin, then hugged him.

"You're being nice because you got so much else that you wanted from this trip, aren't you?" Martin asked.

"No Captain Culver, I see a lot to celebrate. I possess one of the only copies of the pirate Code of the Brethren. I may even turn that into a book, become an author on my own, a pirate author."

"Like the Pyrate Scrybe?"

"Yes, who could be a lady for all you know," Sandra said indignantly. "There's no proof the Scrybe was a man."

"I admit that," Martin replied.

"Do you know what they say about old pirates, especially Jose Gaspar?"

"What do they say?"

"The one saying I was thinking of that describes you to a "T" is this:"

> *"No one decides my fate. I will determine my fate, including when I will live or die."*

"You have proved that over and over again," Sandra said, "to me, to everyone. Jose Gaspar shouted that line as he rode the *Floriblanca's* anchor into the sea. You brought it to life."

"I see what you mean," Martin said as he climbed into the Zodiac lifeboat. Sandra stepped into the Zodiac then stopped before taking a seat.

"Martin look!!"

Martin turned to see a tall sailing boat approaching from the west. A large white catamaran under full sail was bearing down on them, and it was moving fast.

"That boat is going too fast. Is he mad?" Martin asked aloud. "He'll bottom out on the reef!"

Dan called out to them.

"Look out guys, Incoming! That boat is going to run up on the beach. It's pretty big, so watch that mast!"

Martin looked behind the catamaran, noticing what he thought was the same dark sailboat that passed Blue Scorpion Key the night that Sandra almost died returning from the *Cueva de Eva*.

"Do you see the clouds behind the catamaran, Dan?" Martin asked, trying to be evasive.

"Just clouds, not much of a storm. That can't be why the cat is going that fast."

The catamaran cleared the reef, the coral tearing at its hull, screamed up the flat sand toward the hills, finally tipping in slow motion and blowing over onto its side.

"Those people are going to need help Martin. Can you reach them?"

Martin was already on his way, running toward the upended vessel. True to Dan's prediction, the mast did not remain in one position, the stiff breeze that pushed it ashore now billowing the beached sail, spinning the mast towards Martin. He ducked mast and rigging and kept moving forward, hidden in a maze of sailcloth.

As he approached, Martin could see a young girl lying in the sand. He pointed her out to Sandra, who ran up behind him by following his footprints.

"There's a boy over there too, I'm going to check on him," Martin called.

Martin reached the young boy, turned him over, and gently brushed sand from his face.

"Are you ok? Young man are you…wait a minute?"

"I am Enrique. My sister, is she ok?

"Yes, is there anyone else with you?"

"Yes, my abuelo. He is on the boat. Can you reach him? I'm sorry I turned the boat over."

Martin brought his hand up to shade the boy's face.

"Do I know you?" Martin asked. "You resemble my..."

"Martin, it's them, it's them! It's our children!" He turned to see Sandra hugging Elizabeth, smiling until she looked past Martin, horrified at what she saw.

Martin looked behind him to see the same large dark sailboat, now close enough to see the cloaked figure at the bow. From her expression, apparently Sandra could see it too.

"Do you see it?" Enrique asked. "I have been running from that shadow boat all night. It keeps chasing us!"

Martin stood up. He put his hand on Enrique's shoulder.

"Where is your grandfather? Tell me exactly."

"He is in the catamaran berth, in a hammock. He is very sick."

Martin ran for the toppled catamaran, leaping into the net rigging between the two hulls. He climbed like a spider up the webbing until he reached the berth. Looking over the rail, he saw the dark sailboat looming high above him, close to shore.

"Dad, dad, where are you?" Martin called, keeping one

eye on the dark sailboat. "Jack, answer me, you old seadog!"

Martin heard a groan. He opened the door to the berth and found Jack suspended in the hammock, swinging in a reversed position.

"What took you so long?" Jack asked. "I've just been hanging around all topsy turvy. I have all day you know."

Martin ignored Jack's sarcasm.

"Dad, I have to get you out of here. There's a storm coming." Martin did not tell Jack what he really thought.

"There's no hurry," Jack said. "Are the children ok, I hope? Did you find them?"

"Yes, Dad, they're ok. We have them safe on the shore."

"Did Enrique do this? Did he wreck my catamaran?"

"Yes, Dad he did. We need to get out of here. "

"Enrique is a lot like you, Martin. He's a good boy."

"Dad, don't talk like this. You are going to be around for a long time."

"Martin, my time for rushing is over. I have accomplished my mission. I got the children back to you safely."

Jack went into a coughing fit that seemed to go on forever.

"Is she out there?" Jack asked when he stopped coughing. He lay back in the hammock, spent from the effort of his hacking lungs.

"Is who out there?"

"You know who, my ride to the afterlife. She came once for Elizabeth. I sent her packing. Then she gave me a warning. I know you can see her. Is she right outside?"

"Yes, Dad, she is."

"Then I'm ready to go. Give me permission to go."

"Dad, I don't want you to go. How did you find us?"

"I'm not an old seadog for nothing. Everyone who has sailed these waters knows about this island, the Russians, fresh water, the treasure rumors. When you did not come, I decided to come find you. This was the first place on my list after passing the Yucatan. I was headed to old Jeff Lyon's place next. Remember that layout? Anyway, I saw your signal!"

"My signal?"

"Yes, I saw your signal. I don't know what you blew up, but I told Enrique to aim for the smoke column. Whatever you blew up, you did a good job. You should have been a Seabee, or a Seal. Was I right about trying to find you at Jeff's island?"

"Yes, Dad, I own it now. Sandra and I live there. You could live there with us. Don't you want to see Sandra?"

"More than you know," Jack said. "But it's my time, Martin. I feel it. I did my part, I saved those precious children from a world gone mad, a world my generation created. I'm sorry we messed it up. I have to go now."

Martin took his dad's hand. The hand already felt cold.

"Where is she taking you, Dad?"

"To be with your mom, I hope," Jack said. "That would be heaven for me. My life has been hell without her."

Jack started coughing again, too weak to sit up.

"Dad, I love you so much. Thank you for caring for the children," Martin said, hot tears streaming down his face. "I give you permission to go. Mission accomplished. Job well done."

"I love you too, Martin," his father said, closing his eyes as if to sleep. "Say a prayer for me," Jack whispered. "I'll see you again one day. I'll be waiting in Heaven."

Martin bowed his head, but looked directly at his father as he recited the 23rd Psalm as a prayer.

"The Lord is my Shepherd; I shall not want. He makes me to lie down in green pastures, He leads me beside still waters, He restores my soul…"

Continuing to pray, Martin's index finger followed the lines in his father's hand, the way he used to do when he was small.

"And I will dwell in the house of the Lord forever."

By the time Martin finished the prayer, Jack was already with the angels, his body cold and slack.

Martin pulled the sheet up over his father's gently smiling face. He stood up, wiped his eyes, then stepped out of the berth, standing on the trampoline rigging, level with the deck of the dark sailing vessel.

Instantly Jack Culver stood on the dark sailboat waving, with the cloaked figure behind him.

Martin waved, then turned to see Sandra, Enrique and Elizabeth waving too. Dan had his hands up in the air as if to say, "What is going on here? What are we waving at?"

Martin looked back to see the dark sailing vessel leaving, though no sound was heard. Jack Culver remained steadfast, gazing in Martin's direction. As Martin watched, Jack closed his fist over his heart, tapped his chest twice, then saluted, continuing to smile until the ship vanished from view.

Martin carefully climbed down the center webbing to the beach. It dawned on him what his father meant by the closed fist gesture. Jack's diseased heart had been finally made whole.

"I'm glad you waited a bit," Dan said. "The storm clouds I saw have all cleared up now. Just sort of came and went. Are you ready to go?"

"Yes," Martin said, kneeling to hug his children. Sandra smiled broadly, her hands resting on each of their shoulders.

"The storm is over," Martin agreed. "Let's to go home."

THE END

Addendum

Cita Tate, Lead Researcher
Research Librarian, Chief Linguist
International Antiquities Foundation

Premise: Following the death of our colleagues Mary Power, Rebekah Jayne Osgood, and Carter Hall, the age-old question arises: What happens after a person dies?

While we each may have settled in our hearts and minds our final destination, limited hard evidence exists for the human journey from physical body to the spiritual afterlife. This proposal addresses the aforementioned lack.

Proposal: This research examines Angelic beings of the Bible to Greek mythology, as well as Asian influences, including spirit guides that appear in the art and artifacts of among cultures across the globe. All testify to guides of a spiritual nature leading into the next life. Direct observation, however, records only the dying moments of loved ones and friends, without insight.

From whence do these myths and artifacts originate? From the common memory of a forgotten era? Or from a common experience commemorated in the artworks cited?

Who is to say what is true or real in this context. Personal belief plays a large part.

In the interim, consider your own personal belief in the concept of an afterlife spirit guide to heaven. Ask yourself these questions:
- Would my afterlife guide be known to me?
- Would my afterlife guide be visible to me?
- Would my afterlife guide know my family?
- Would my afterlife guide be known to my family?
- Would my afterlife guide be visible to my family?

---

*"The Lost Library of Alexandria", Novel 5, TCMS

About the Author

Malcom Massey primarily writes "The Martin Culver Series", action adventures written with a healthy pour of archaeology, topped with a twist of CIA thriller, shaken, not stirred.

Meeting both famed treasure hunter Mel Fisher in Key West, Florida and undersea explorer Jacques Cousteau in Norfolk, Virginia heavily influenced Malcom's decision to write international adventure novels.

Malcom prefers to write novels that tie the past to the present, weaving modern technology against ancient history and artifacts for exciting and suspenseful adventures. He mostly reads history, archaeology and mythology, along with some scientific texts and journals.

Malcom still writes and lives near the coast.

Find more novels in The Martin Culver Series here:

http://www.amazon.com/author/malcommassey

Made in United States
Orlando, FL
21 June 2023